Quid Pro Quo

Sherryl D. Hancock

Published by Vulpine Press in the United Kingdom in 2018

ISBN: 978-1-912701-46-9

Cover by Claire Wood

Cover photo credit: Tirzah D. Hancock

www.vulpine-press.com

Thank you to the Sacramento Front Street Shelter for teaching me about dogs and for all the incredible work you do! Rescue animals make the very best pets!

Also in the WeHo series:

When Love Wins

When Angels Fall

Break in the Storm

Turning Tables

Marking Time

Jet Blue

Water Under the Bridge

Vendetta

Gray Skies

Everything to Everyone

Lightning Strykes

In Plain Sight

Prologue

"I think I'll take him back," Cody said, standing up from the ground and taking the leash of the small dog she'd been working with.

Shenin smiled up at her. "Okay."

They'd done good work that morning; Cody Falco, for all her impatience elsewhere, was very focused when it came to working with the timid dogs at the shelter. Shenin knew it was good therapy for Cody, as much as it was good therapy for her and Skyler Boché as well; they all had issues to work through, and doing it while helping shy dogs get adopted always seemed like a perfect fit.

It was a nice cool morning at the shelter; the Los Angeles summer heat finally seemed to be abating. The crisp mornings of fall were on the way. It seemed to put everyone in a better mood. Shenin stood up, stretching her back, knowing she shouldn't sit as long as she had been on the hard pavement.

"Ugh," she groaned as her back protested. She grinned at Skyler. "Guess I know what Ty's gonna be doing later this afternoon."

"Working out all the knots in your back that you just put in?" Skyler asked, even as the dog she was working with licked her face, making her chuckle softly.

"Pretty much. And complaining that I do it on purpose..." Shenin said with a grin.

Things between Shenin and Tyler had gotten so much better in the last year and a half. Their relationship had been tested a couple of years before when Shenin pulled away from Tyler, the absolute love of her life. Tyler had been at a loss as to how to deal with Shenin's post-traumatic stress from a war-time abduction and injury. There had been much more to the story than Tyler had known. Tyler was a captain with the Air Force and a member of their security force, as Shenin had been before she was hurt in a car accident. She was also very protective of her wife, and Shenin had known that some of the details of her abduction, very specifically her rape by her captors, would kill Tyler. Keeping the secret had almost killed Shenin, and just about destroyed their relationship. Fortunately, things had come to a head and that had given them the ability to get through it. Between counseling and therapy with things like timid shelter dogs, Shenin was dealing with her trauma and life-long battle with depression.

****

Kai Temple walked through the shelter with the law enforcement liaison she'd met to discuss the viability of retraining shelter dogs as assets to law enforcement units.

"So you've had success with animals like this before?" the liaison asked, smiling up at the taller woman.

Kai Temple was an impressive sight. She stood five feet nine inches, with long, straight jet black hair usually pulled back into a ponytail, and dark, almond-shaped eyes. She had a very attractive face, with an exotic look to her features. Her skin was darkly tanned and smooth; it was impossible to guess that she was actually thirty-nine years old—she looked much younger. She also had an impressive build of solid muscle. She wasn't overly bulky, but her highly toned shape was definitely hinted at by her close-fitting white thermal shirt with the sleeves pushed up. Her long, muscular legs were emphasized nicely by her faded jeans. It was obvious that Kai Temple took excellent care of her body.

"Yeah, in Afghanistan we were able to—" Kai's statement was cut off by the radio call.

"We have a loose dog from isolation, I Building! Loose dog from isolation, I Building!"

Kai turned toward the area cited, scanning the space. She immediately saw the large Rottweiler walking down the side of the fencing. She let out a loud whistle as she started to run over.

Cody had left the small, fenced-off "play yard" to take back the dog she'd been working with. She'd just turned past isolation and was heading down the row toward the strays building when she heard the call. She turned to look around; she knew she was close to the I Building. She heard a sharp whistle just as the Rottweiler came around the corner. The dog let out a loud bark and started toward her. Cody could see that it was extremely agitated; its hair was standing up on its back, a clear sign. She backed up, putting the small dog she was returning into a kennel that happened to be open. Her main concern was the dog, not her own safety. The Rottweiler was further agitated by the other dogs barking at it from nearby kennels—suddenly it growled, baring its teeth, and started running for Cody. Cody backed up into the fence, freezing up in her fear.

Just as the Rottweiler would have leapt for her throat, Cody heard a sharp command.

"*Nein! Platz!*" The voice giving the command was deep, intense, and the Rottweiler responded immediately, stopping and lying down. A moment later it started panting.

Cody was sure she was going to pass out from relief. She looked up and saw a tall woman with a dark complexion walking toward her, her eyes searching her.

"Are you okay?" Kai asked.

Cody nodded, blowing her breath out in relief as she leaned forward, breathing heavily. "How did you know to do that? That was like German, right?"

Kai chuckled. "Well, I tried 'Stop' and 'Down' in English first—you probably just didn't hear me. But he's a Rottie, so I figured he might know German commands."

Cody leaned back and dropped her head against the fence. "Thank God you were here."

"You froze up," Kai said. "You can't do that around these big guys." She knelt to the side and put her hand out to the Rottweiler, which immediately sniffed it.

"So you know dogs?" Cody asked, still eyeing the Rottweiler cautiously.

Kai grinned. "Yeah. Worked with them in the Marines."

Kai took a leather leash that had been hanging around her neck and put it on the Rottweiler, then said, "*Steh.*" The Rottweiler stood, his big head turned up to Kai.

"I'm Kai," she said to Cody, extending her hand.

"Cody." She nodded. "Thank you."

"Just gotta be careful with these big boys." Kai smiled with very white, perfectly even teeth, her dark eyes twinkling.

"That's why I work with the ones that size," Cody said, pointing at the small dog safely in the kennel.

Kai raised an eyebrow. "Put her in there and didn't get in with her?"

"Didn't think about it, really," Cody said, grimacing.

Kai nodded. "Happens to the best of us." She held out her forearm, pointing to a half-inch scar on the inside. "First encounter with an Afghan Shepherd trained to kill American soldiers," she said, grinning. "Got too close and froze when he warned me off."

"Ouch," Cody said, closing one eye and wincing.

Kai chuckled. "Yeah, it hurt. He bit all the way through my uniform sleeve."

"How'd that turn out?"

Kai grinned. "He lives with me now."

"Guess you didn't take it too personally."

"It's never personal. It's fear—it's always fear, which breeds aggression."

Cody nodded.

"Oh my God, Cody, are you okay!" Shenin exclaimed as she and Skyler came around the corner.

They'd both heard the all clear on the radio from one of the vet techs and had come out to see what had happened. The law enforcement liaison Kai had been working with them had explained.

"Yeah, I'm good," Cody said, smiling. "Shen, Skyler, this is Kai…" She trailed off as she realized she didn't know Kai's last name.

"Temple," Kai said. "Kai Temple." She held her hand out to both Skyler and Shenin.

"Kai's the reason I'm okay," Cody said. "Otherwise I would have been a Rottie chew toy." She smiled down at the dog, who was watching everyone with interest.

Shenin and Skyler looked surprised, then started to nod.

"Thank you," Shenin said to Kai. "That could have been bad."

"It could have," Kai said. "But it wasn't."

"Thanks to you," Skyler added, nodding.

Kai inclined her head, which put Cody in the mind of something Remington LaRoché would do, and that gave her another thought.

"Hey, have you ever been to The Club?" she asked, easily recognizing Kai as "family"—the term the LGBT community used for fellow gays.

Kai nodded. "A few times. Why?"

"Well, our friend Memphis is spinning tonight," Cody said. "And I'd like to buy you a drink, and I'm sure my wife would love to thank you for keeping me hole-free," she added, grinning.

Kai chuckled. "Okay, I'll be there. What time?"

"Say nine?"

"You got it."

Later that night Kai walked into The Club and was immediately greeted by Cody, who was holding hands with a beautiful blonde with big blue eyes—her wife.

"Kai, this is McKenna," Cody said.

McKenna reached up to hug Kai, smiling. "Thank you for saving my girl for me."

Kai grinned. "I was saving the dog too. If he'd bitten your wife, they would have put him down immediately."

"All about the dog…" Cody said, smiling as she shook her head.

"Always."

"Kai?" came a voice from behind her.

Kai turned around to see Remington LaRoché standing there with her girlfriend, Wynter.

"Hey!" Kai said, smiling widely as she shook Remington's hand before hugging Wynter, kissing her on the cheek. "How are you two?"

"Good," Remington said. "I didn't think you came here," she added, her look pointed.

"I don't, usually. But Cody invited me."

"'Cause she quite literally saved my neck today at the shelter," Cody said.

"How?" Remington asked as they walked toward the rest of the group.

"There was a Rottie loose, and he was getting aggressive," Kai said.

"Yeah, thinking about killing me is how I saw it," Cody added with a grin.

Kai laughed. "Nah." She shook her head. "He was just trying to show you who he thought was boss."

"And you showed him you were?" Remington asked.

Kai smiled. "Always the alpha, never the beta."

Remington laughed.

"What does that mean?" Wynter asked.

"It means there's no room for second best," Kai said, her expression serious.

"I see…" Wynter said, smiling.

Cody introduced Kai to her mothers, Lyric and Savanna. They were both effusive in their thanks for keeping Cody safe.

"So, how do you know Remi?" Cody asked after she'd introduced Kai to the rest of the group.

"She trained me," Remington said.

Cody looked back at Kai, shock momentarily evident on her face, but then she took in Kai's appearance. She was wearing faded jeans, black leather two-inch-heeled boots, and a black Oxford tucked into her jeans and open at the throat. Around her neck she wore a thick silver chain with a dog tag hanging from it; the silver pendant depicted a bronze winged dragon. She also wore a thick-banded black watch at her wrist and a series of silver rings on her fingers. What Cody saw now that she was looking for it was the width of Kai's shoulders and the way her waist tapered in; there was no appearance of fragility about the other woman.

"You're a trainer?" McKenna asked, expressing the surprise Cody hadn't.

Kai chuckled. "Yeah."

"But you know how to handle dogs?" Lyric asked.

"That too."

"Kai!" Quinn called as she and Xandy walked up to the group.

"Hey!" Kai exclaimed, reaching over to shake Quinn's hand. "Hey there, pretty girl," she said to Xandy, smiling as she reached over to hug her gently.

"Hi, Kai," Xandy said, smiling up at her.

Cody gave them an odd look. "Okay…"

"Kai trained me that month before the fight, while we were still on the tour," Remington said, referring to the tour Wynter and Xandy had been performing on while Remington and Quinn acted as their bodyguards.

"Oh—yeah." Cody nodded. "That makes sense."

"So she knows Memphis too then?" McKenna asked.

"Well, yeah." Remington looked at Kai. "You met Memphis, right?"

Kai looked pensive, shrugging. "Dunno, don't remember."

Remington pointed to a girl with white-blonde hair in a black hoodie in the DJ booth at the front of the dance floor.

"Oh! Yeah—yeah, I met her," Kai said. "She's the one that ended with all that shit coming down, right?" she asked, her tone softening.

Remington and Quinn nodded, both looking pained. Kai was referring to Memphis' confrontation with a cult that had been out to get her, a group that her mother had brought a five-year-old Memphis into before trying to marry her off to their "prophet" at the age of sixteen. Memphis had been caught and assaulted by members of the cult, including the prophet himself. Remington and Quinn, who were Memphis' self-appointed protectors, had been desperate to get her back. In the end, help had come from a surprising source in the form of the California Attorney General Midnight Chevalier and some of her loyal former employees, all cops. It had been a rough time for all of them, but they'd managed to rescue Memphis and had arrested the prophet and all of his members who'd been involved in the assault.

"She's okay now, though, right?" Kai asked.

"She's doing a lot better," Remington said.

Kai nodded. "Good to hear."

It became evident over the next hour that Kai was very definitely good friends with Remington, and had obviously become friends with Wynter, Quinn, and Xandy during her time with the tour. Kai being an ex-Marine was also discussed, and how, like Remington, she was a reserve. Kashena, who was an ex-Marine herself, quickly bonded with Kai as well. Kai was an easy inclusion in the group. That was tested an hour later when she froze while looking toward the front door.

"Ah hell…" Kai muttered, grimacing.

"What?" Remington asked as she followed Kai's gaze, then grimaced herself.

"What?" Wynter said, looking between the two women.

"The reason I don't come here just walked in," Kai said, her tone low. She glanced over at Remington. "I'm gonna go outside and smoke."

Remington nodded as her eyes tracked the blonde who had just walked into the club. She was almost as tall as Remington and Kai, at five foot seven inches. She had sharply cut cheek bones and ice-blue eyes. She also carried an air of superiority about her that apparently hadn't abated since getting out of the Marines.

"Who is that?" Wynter asked Remington.

"Her name's Kathy. She was a colonel in the Marines and Kai's commanding officer at one point."

"And that's why Kai is avoiding her?"

"Kai's avoiding her because she raked Kai's heart over the coals so many times it's not even funny," Remington said. "And she knows Kai's here—that's who she's looking for."

"How does she know she's here?" Wynter asked.

"She has friends that probably told her, but she comes here a lot, which is why Kai doesn't usually… and she's spotted her," Remington said, seeing Kathy look toward the patio where Kai was smoking and already pacing. "Be right back." She leaned down to kiss Wynter on the lips.

Remington got out to the patio slightly ahead of Kathy and headed over to Kai. "Incoming," she said with a pointed look.

Kai turned around and glanced over Remington's shoulder, rolling her eyes as she did and shaking her head.

"Don't let her fuck with you," Remington said quietly.

"Easier said than done." Kai already looked like she was affected by Kathy's presence.

Remington grimaced, then turned to look at the former colonel. Her eyes narrowed as she walked past her and back into the bar.

"Kai…" Kathy said, reaching out to touch her arm.

"Don't," Kai said, shifting just out of Kathy's reach.

"Really? You're going to be this petty now?"

Kai looked back at her, her expression reflecting annoyance at the rebuke. She leaned back against the wall of the club, putting her foot up behind her casually, lifting her cigarette to her lips and taking a long drag. She blew it out a minute later, her eyes narrowing in the curl of the smoke.

"My feelings always seem petty to you," she said wryly. "I wonder why that is?"

"That's a bit of an over-generalization, don't you think?" Kathy said condescendingly.

"I think I don't fucking have to care what you think anymore, Kat, so just go away."

"Don't be like that," Kathy said, moving closer.

Kai's chin came up immediately. "You know, I don't usually hit women, but I might make an exception for you." Her tone was conversational, but her expression was far from casual.

"You won't," Kathy said, undaunted. "You won't because you'd rather fuck me than hit me…" She slid her hand up Kai's chest, feeling the other woman shudder. "See? You miss me. Just admit it so we can move forward."

"Still married?" Kai asked sharply.

"We're getting divorced," Kathy said, as if that made everything okay.

Kai gave a short laugh, shaking her head. "Yeah, I've heard that one before." Kathy had said as much about her husband, back when they were both in the Middle East and their romance had been hot and heavy, or so Kai had thought.

Tossing aside her cigarette, she grabbed Kathy's hand at the wrist and pointedly removed it from her, staring down into her eyes.

"Get your hands off of me. I don't belong to you anymore," she said, and with that shoved Kathy away.

Kathy stepped back, her eyes flaring. She wasn't used to not getting what she wanted.

"You will come back to me, Kai," she said sharply. "And when you do, I'm going to make you sorry you pulled this little power play." She narrowed her eyes in the nasty way Kai remembered so well. "I was, am, and will always be your superior, Kai Marou Temple—don't ever forget that." Kathy pivoted on her heel and marched back into the club.

Kai winced as the door slammed, then banged her head on the wall a couple of times, praying to the powers that be that Kathy wasn't right.

"Fuck!" she yelled, hitting the back of her head on the concrete once more.

She didn't see the blond woman standing just off to the side, who had been doing her best not to overhear everything that had been said. Nor did she see the grimace the woman made when she banged her head on the concrete.

Finley Taylor did her best to leave the area without Kai Temple noticing her. Fortunately, she succeeded.

Chapter 1

"Fin!" called one of the nurses.

Finley craned her neck around to look at the woman, who was gesturing at the small brunette practically bouncing with energy. Nodding, Finley motioned to the girl to come over, even as she sighed. This one was becoming a lot of work now.

"Hi, honey!" the girl said, bounding up to her and kissing her lips.

"Hey, Jenny," Finley said, making sure her voice reflected her chagrin at Jenny showing up at the ER where she worked. "This really isn't a good time…"

"But you said we were going out today," Jenny said, pouting prettily, as she dragged the toe of her heeled pump on the pavement.

"I got called in, Jenny. It's cold and flu season—a lot of staff are out," Finley explained patiently, trying her best not to be completely annoyed.

This girl was particularly cute, with her long, curly brown hair with boatloads of blond highlights. She was dressed in amicro mini dress with thigh-high black-and-white-striped tights and black high heels. There was some fairly spectacular smooth, tanned thigh show-ing, and Finley found it somewhat distracting. The girl was sexy all the time, and Finley knew she was using her for exactly that. She pretty much used them all for sex, never bothering to get too deep with any of them. Most of the girls she ended up with wouldn't understand ninety-eight percent of what she'd say if she actually tried to talk to them about more than clothes, hair, and/or makeup.

"But..." Jenny began, looking at Finley through her bangs. Her pretty blue eyes, heavily made up, were glassy with tears.

"Come on, don't do that," Finley said, knowing full well the girl was laying it on thick. "You know I gotta work."

"You always gotta work."

"That's what it's like dating a doctor, hon." Finley grimaced mentally as she saw a beatific smile light Jenny's face up.

"We're dating?" Jenny asked, her voice painfully hopeful.

"Well, you know..." Finley said, keeping her tone casual, even as she turned her back to Jenny and made faces at herself. "Like seeing a doctor... you know, like that."

Turning back around, Finley could see she hadn't gotten out of that one. *Damnit, damnit damnit!* The last thing she wanted was for this girl to think they were dating—it meant she'd want even more time from her that she wasn't willing to give.

"We'll go out sometime next week, okay?" she said, smiling.

"You promise?" Jenny said, already looking for commitments.

"I'll call you," Finley said, avoiding promising anything. "And maybe I can buy you something to make it up to you... okay?" She knew the offer would entice Jenny.

"Really?" Jenny asked, her blue eyes lighting up like it was Christmas morning.

Finley smiled, nodding. "But I gotta get back inside before I freeze!" She put her hands inside her blue sweatshirt with Cedars Sinai on the breast pocket.

Ten minutes later and an orgasm for Jenny achieved easily enough around the side of the building in a dark corner, Finley walked back into the ER.

"When you gonna stop that shit?" asked Jackie, the heavyset black nurse who had known Finley for the ten years that she'd been at Cedars Sinai and considered herself Finley's "other mama."

Finley looked guilty for a moment, wondering if Jackie somehow knew about the quick and dirty sex at the back of the hospital. "Stop what shit?" she asked as she went to pick up the charts for the three patients they'd taken in in the few minutes she'd been outside.

"Datin' those pretty little nothings," Jackie said, making a sucking sound through her teeth when Finley only grinned. "Don't you grin at me like that, girlie! I'm serious!"

Finley turned to lean against the counter next to where Jackie sat, crossing her arms in front of her chest. "It's easier, Jacks. They don't require a lot of work."

Jackie gave her a narrowed look. "Work's part of a real relationship, Finley Ann Taylor."

Finley rolled her eyes. "Who says I want a real relationship?"

"Girl!" Jackie exclaimed. "The Good Lord put us on this Earth for one reason and one reason only. To find love!"

Finley laughed, shaking her head. "I know, I know."

"So you gotta get to it. Those beautiful looks aren't going to last forever, ya know." Jackie circled her finger to indicate Finley's face.

Finley Taylor was a beautiful woman, of that there was no

doubt, with naturally curly honey-blond hair like spun silk and brandy-colored eyes in a beautiful, finely boned face, and pouty lips and a curvy but fit body that could have been sculpted by Botticelli himself.

"Jesus, Jackie, I'm thirty-four—can I have a life first?" Finley said, rolling her eyes.

"Don't you want babies?"

"Oh God, don't start that!" Finley shook her head. "You know not all women actually want kids, right?"

"Oh, come on, you'd make such beautiful babies!"

"Like I have time for that. Any woman I'd have kids with would have to have the kid."

"But then it wouldn't get your beautiful genes."

Finley grinned. "Yeah, I could live with that."

"But your mama would just love grandbabies…" Jackie said, her tone changing slightly.

"Like I care what she wants. Besides, she'd want me to have a kid with a man, she's okay with me dating women, but she doesn't get the concept of in vitro or any of that stuff, Jackie, and me with a man… that ain't happening!"

"Well, none of these little pop tarts you're dating would have a baby."

"And I never said I wanted a baby, Jacks," Finley countered. "I gotta go check on patients," she added, giving her dirty look.

Jackie stared after the young woman, shaking her head. The girl was far too headstrong for her own good sometimes.

****

"You did what?" Kai asked the blonde sitting across from her in the passenger seat of her car.

"I kind of used his credit card…" the girl replied, cringing.

Kai dropped her head back against the headrest, banging it a couple of times. "He's gonna go ballistic. Jesus, Cass, why?"

There was an impatient honk behind them. Kai threw her hand up in a gesture of acknowledgment. They were sitting in a bright green Mercedes-AMG GT R, with its sleek lines and low-slung appearance. The car was parked at the curb at the Los Angeles International Airport, known as LAX.

Cassiana Temple stared at her half-sister. She was still stunned by Kai's appearance. She hadn't seen any recent pictures of Kai; she'd only ever seen photos of her when she'd been younger, around twelve, and she hadn't looked anything like she did now. Gone were the gangly arms, replaced by lean, sharply defined muscle. The legs that had looked long and skinny were now well muscled, outlined in tight, faded jeans and sharply bent at the knees as Kai lounged comfortably behind the wheel of her sports car. Also gone was any sign of the awkwardness that had been apparent in Kai's younger pictures.

This woman looked anything but awkward; in fact, she seemed extremely comfortable in her own skin. It was something Cassiana longed for. At sixteen, she felt so completely out of place in her life, and Kai had been the only person she could turn to, so she'd acted on impulse and stolen their father's credit card to pay for a flight to Los Angeles from Washington DC

"I had to get out of there, Kai Marou…" she said tremulously.

"Why, what happened?" Kai asked, narrowing her eyes slightly.

Cassiana looked nervous suddenly, shaking her head. The guy behind them honked again.

"Are ya fuckin' kiddin' me, dude!" Kai yelled, gesturing for him to go around her. There was space on the curb in front of her car— the guy was just being an asshole, and she wasn't in the mood for it.

"Cass, what happened?" Kai knew how volatile their father was, and was worried that he'd actually lost his mind and gotten physical with the girl.

Cassiana picked at the stitching on the leather seat, her eyes downcast. "He caught me…"

"With?" Kai asked, thinking if Cassiana was about to say "a boy," the next call she'd get would be one asking her to go bail her father out of jail for murder.

"A girl," Cassiana said, shocking the hell right out of Kai.

"I'm sorry?"

Cassiana raised her head, her stare accusing. "How can you act like that? You're gay!"

Kai laughed, shaking her head. "I'm just thinking that history is repeating itself, that's all."

"What do you mean?"

"I mean, Dad caught me in that same room with a girl when I was fourteen."

"Oh…" Cassiana said, her eyes widening. "How did he react?"

Kai gave a short bark of humorless laughter. "I was in a military boarding school two days later."

Cassiana had turned pale. "What?"

There was a sharp rap on Kai's window. She glanced over and saw the guy from the car behind. He was short and stocky. Kai narrowed her eyes as she opened her window.

"You can't park here, lady. This isn't your gab-fest parking," he snapped.

Kai looked back at him for a long moment, much like a cat examines at a mouse. Then she reached for the door handle, climbed out of the low-slung Mercedes, and stood looking down at the guy, who only came up to her chin.

"Do you see the curb space in front of my vehicle?" she asked evenly as she gestured to the open area.

"That's not the point! You rich bitches think you can park your Mercedes anywhere you want. I'm in a hurry!"

Kai narrowed her eyes dangerously, then slowly turned her head to the truck he was driving—predictably, it was a piece of crap on wheels. She looked back at the man.

"Sir," she said, her tone still even, "if you were really in a hurry, and not just being an asshole for what you think I have that you don't have, you'd have moved the fuck around me five minutes ago, and not come bitching at me." She pointed a long-fingered hand at the end of a well-muscled arm, on full display in her tank top, at his truck. "So move that piece of shit before I take that horn of yours and wrap it around your neck. You got it?"

The guy looked back at her, his eyes blazing, and she could see he was itching for a fight. She canted her head slightly with a grin that told him she had no problem beating him senseless even though she was dressed for a night out rather than a brawl. His gaze swept over her—she definitely looked like she could back up what she was saying.

He turned around to walk back to his truck, muttering, "Fuckin' dykes…"

"We won't fuck you," Kai said, loudly enough for anyone nearby to hear. "But that's the problem, isn't it?"

She heard people laughing as she got back into her car, looking over at her half-sister, who was laughing too.

"Wow, you really told him," Cassiana said.

Kai watched as the man pulled around her car and parked at the curb in front of her. "Guys like that are a dime a dozen," she said, curling her lips in derision. She grinned. "Let's get out of here before the cops decide to come hassle me next."

They went to a restaurant in West Hollywood called Norm's. It was a diner-style place, and the staff seemed to know Kai even though she obviously didn't eat much of the kind of food they served. Kai ordered a Greek chicken salad with dressing on the side, while Cassiana ate like a teenager, ordering a burger, fries, onion rings, a shake, and a Coke.

"How can you eat that?" Cassiana asked, giving her half-sister a disgusted look.

"I could ask you the same question," Kai replied mildly.

"Dude, it's all-American food!"

"Which is why more than a third of Americans are considered obese," Kai said with a pointed look.

"Do I look fat?" Cassiana asked, gesturing to herself.

"No," Kai said, grinning. "You got lucky with the genes."

"Uh-huh." Cassiana rolled her eyes. "You haven't seen my mom."

"No, I haven't," Kai said, her tone changing slightly.

"Sorry." Cassiana knew it was likely a sore spot.

Kai sighed. "It's okay, Cass. It's not surprising at all to me that my dad cheated on my mother. She's such a doormat he could probably become the next Hitler and she'd be okay with it."

"But still…"

Kai chuckled softly, her tone far from humorous. "Cass, you'll find that our father and I aren't exactly on the same page on most things, least of all relationships and what's appropriate."

Cassiana's mother, an administrative clerk for Kai's father, had had an affair with General Marou Temple for two years while he was stationed over in Iraq. Cassiana had been the result. Fourteen years later Cassiana's mother had shown up on the Temple doorstep, demanding money from Marou for his daughter's child support. A nasty court case had been avoided by Marou paying Cassiana's mother off and taking Cassiana into their home, much to the disappointment of Kai's mother, Cho Temple. Not that it had been enough to get Cho to divorce Marou. Nothing was ever enough for that, not even shipping their only daughter off to military boarding school for being gay.

Kai had only met Cassiana through email and chat because Cassiana had found her contact address in their mother's stuff and started emailing her, wanting to reach out to her only sister. They'd had long conversations about how Cho treated her "like a bug in her house." Their father had no idea how to handle girls, and so he didn't really deal with her either.

"Did he really send you to military school because you were gay?" Cassiana asked nervously.

Kai nodded seriously. "Yup. I never lived at home again."

"So you graduated from that school?"

"Yeah."

"Which school was it?"

"RMA—Randolph-Macon Academy in Virginia."

"I've heard of that place…" Cassiana looked scared. "Do you think he's going to do that to me?"

Kai shrugged. "I have no idea, but I wouldn't be too surprised if he tried."

"Tried?"

Kai looked at the girl. She was small, only about five foot four inches, and weighed perhaps 110 pounds, with no muscle whatsoever. When Kai had been fourteen, she was already taller than Cassiana and had some muscle tone because of her need to be out of the house—she spent a lot of time running.

"Do you think you could make it in a place like RMA?" Kai asked.

"Hell no!" Cassiana exclaimed, startling the people around them.

Kai grinned. "Okay, well, then we'll have to talk him out of it."

"You'd help me?"

Kai looked pensive for a moment, but nodded. "Yeah, I'd have to."

"Why?"

Kai looked at her for a long moment. "Because I don't want your life to become like mine was."

"Was it that bad?"

"It wasn't good."

"So you're a dyke?" her platoon leader asked her first day.

"Sir?" she asked, fortunately conditioned from birth to address people in authority with respect.

"A fucking dyke, Temple—you know, a cunt that likes other cunts," the man said, getting right in her face.

She could hear the other plebes snickering. She narrowed her eyes, her temper flaring.

"Oh, you mean a girl that thinks your dick is too small to be useful," she said, her tone as disrespectful as she could make it.

She was actually stunned by the punch to the gut that had her doubling over in pain; she should have been ready for the knee to the face that put her on the ground, but she just wasn't. Foolishly, she'd thought her dad's name would protect her here. She had no idea that he'd been the one who'd ordered them to get the idea of her being a lesbian out of her head once and for all.

It was just the beginning of the abuse she would take over the next six months. It was abuse that would leave her broken, bleeding and bruised from head to toe. All the while she continued to level as much hate at her detractors as they leveled at her.

When the summer break came, she refused to go home, even if her father and mother would have allowed her to at that point. Instead she spent her summer hitting the gym, running, lifting, and increasing her speed and strength. It wasn't in her to be a victim for long.

When the next school year started, the first man that got in her face about being a dyke was put down and put down hard by a fifteen-year-old girl. He never lived that down. A few other boys and men made the same mistake; they all got the same treatment. People learned quickly not to fuck with Kai Temple. The final act of defiance that cemented her as a legend in the school was when she walked into the lunchroom wearing only a jog bra and yoga pants, the muscles she'd gained over the last nine months on full display. She also had the word DYKE written across her forehead in black. She went up to the stage, climbing up and standing there until every eye in the room was on her.

"Anyone want to try me, come try now," she said, holding out her arms.

There was some shuffling of feet. One of the cockier young men, a senior, got up and walked over to her.

"I'll fuck you, if that's what you need," he said, his voice full of confidence.

His comment gained a number of snickers and some laughs as well. Kai looked him dead in the eye and said, "If you think you can, come try."

He stepped closer, and she hopped down off the stage and instantly moved into a fighter's stance. "Come at me, boy."

He charged, and she put him down with one punch, shocking everyone in the lunchroom.

"Anyone else?" she asked, secretly hoping no one else would try it, because she was fairly sure she'd just broken a couple of bones in her

hand—not that her expression showed the pain.

No one moved. No one made a sound.

She scanned the group, pausing on the individuals who'd tortured her previously, including instructors. Many of them dropped their eyes; others met her look and nodded, like they understood she was done putting up with abuse. She walked out of the room and immediately went to the infirmary to have her hand looked at, cursing herself all the way for not taping up.

"What have you done to yourself?" asked the nurse, a pretty black girl whose name tag read Kerry.

"Put a stop to getting my ass beat regularly," Kai said offhandedly.

Kerry held her hand out. "Let me see."

Kai put her hand out, and Kerry grimaced instantly. "Girl..." she breathed. "You're supposed to hurt them, not yourself."

"Wasn't really the plan," Kai said, grinning engagingly.

Kerry canted her head. "Did ya have a plan?"

"Sure..." Kai let her voice trail off to indicate that she hadn't really planned anything—she'd just needed to put a stop to her harassment.

"You have got to control that temper of yours," Kerry said, gently holding Kai's hand as she applied antiseptic to her cut knuckles.

"Why?" Kai snapped, yanking her hand away. "No one tells these guys they need to control their fucking mouths!"

Kerry looked at her critically. "No, they don't, and no one ever will, but you'll break every bone in your hand punching them all in the mouth—for what?"

"Satisfaction," Kai said defiantly.

"But you're smarter than that."

"What makes you think that?"

Kerry shook her head, taking Kai's hand again and continuing to clean it. She took her time wrapping it in an ACE bandage, without saying another word. Kai remained silent, refusing to ask Kerry what she'd meant.

When Kerry sat back, Kai got up. Kerry stood too, taking Kai's face in her hands and staring into her eyes.

"You are a smart, beautiful girl. You can do more if you use your brain, and not just your brawn. Brawn is what men use—brains are what we girls have that they don't. Use that."

With that Kerry kissed Kai on the cheek.

Kai remembered that statement for many years to come.

As Kai pulled out of the restaurant parking lot her phone rang. She hit hands-free. "Hello?"

"Hey…" It was a woman's voice. "I thought you were coming out tonight?"

"Hi, Sandy." Kai grinned. "I was planning on it." She glanced over at Cassiana. "But I kind of ended up with a surprise house guest. So I'm not gonna make it, sorry."

"Is she cute?" Sandy asked.

"She's my sister."

"Then she's gotta be cute—bring her along!"

"She's sixteen," Kai said pointedly.

"Oh," Sandy said, sounding circumspect. "Bring her anyway!"

"Uh, no," Kai said, smiling, as Cassiana glanced over at her with a wide grin.

"Spoilsport," Sandy said.

"That's me."

"Well, your fine ass needs to call me—we need to hook up."

"Uh-huh." Kai rolled her eyes; her sister was hearing more than she really needed to. "I'll call you."

"You better! Or I'll come find you."

They hung up a moment later.

"She sounds, um, interested…" Cassiana commented.

"Uh-huh," Kai repeated, grinning.

"So how much play does this car get you?"

"Watch your mouth," Kai said, narrowing her eyes at her sister.

"Sorry," Cassiana said, grinning. "How much vagina does this car get you?"

Kai looked over at her sharply, then shook her head. "The smartass thing must be genetic," she said wryly.

"Or do you have a girlfriend, or something? You never talked about anyone specific, so…"

"No, I don't have a girlfriend."

"Are you, like, getting it from everyone, or what?"

"What makes you think I'm getting any at all?"

"Kai, you might be my half-sister and all, but I know a hot lesbian when I see one, and you're hot, so you're getting it and probably plenty."

Kai shook her head, wondering how in the world she had gotten into this. "I'm not having this conversation with you."

"KaiMarou, you are so straitlaced!"

"How many times are we going to cover the 'KaiMarou' thing?" Kai said. "Marou is my middle name."

Cassiana laughed. "And I've been calling you KaiMarou for two years now, so get over it."

Kai rolled her eyes, shaking her head.

"So, speaking of hot lesbians, are there any younger ones around here?"

"Are you even sure you're a lesbian?"

"Uh, the girl that Dad caught me with had me halfway home when he walked in…"

Kai made a noise in the back of her throat, then grinned. "Yeah, he has a bad habit of knowing just when to walk in and screw up any chances of an orgasm…"

Cassiana laughed. "He messed you up too?"

"Oh yeah," Kai said, shaking her head. "S'okay, she caught up with me the next day at school and finished the job, in a bathroom stall no less."

"Holy shit! You must have been pretty hot even then."

"No, she was just bound and determined not to have a bad date on her record. She was a senior."

"So like, four years older than you?" Cassiana looked impressed.

"Well, three, but yeah. What was the deal with the girl you were with?"

"Oh, she was my age and really hot, a new girl from California."

"Where all the fruits and nuts come from, right?" Kai remembered that was what they'd thought when she was in school.

"Hey, my sister's from California at this point, so don't be talking stuff…" Cassiana said, grinning.

Kai smiled back. "And your sister's one of the fruits."

"And she's also awesome," Cassiana said seriously.

Kai looked over, her eyes searching the young girl's face.

"You are, Kai," Cassiana said. "You're the only one in this family that accepted me and treats me like I matter."

"You do matter, Cass."

"Not to them," Cassiana said, gesturing nebulously toward Washington, DC. "To them I'm just something to be tolerated so our dad doesn't have to pay my mom any more money."

Kai grimaced. "I'm sorry. I hoped that it was just because of what I was…" She shook her head. "I guess some people just shouldn't have kids at all."

"I'm just glad I met you," Cassiana said, her dark eyes, so like Kai's, glazing with tears. "If I hadn't, I don't know what I would have done."

"Did you know you were gay all along?"

Cassiana shrugged. "I knew I wasn't interested in boys like my friends were. I guess I thought I was just a late bloomer or something.

30

But then when you told me you were gay it made me wonder... I started looking stuff up on the Internet and reading all kinds of stories about how people figured out they were gay."

Kai nodded. "You're lucky that you have that nowadays. When I was younger than you, I had no idea what was going on with me. What I knew was that I was attracted to girls the way the girls were attracted to the boys... That senior wasn't my first."

"How old were you the first time you were with a girl?"

"The first time I was with a girl I was thirteen. She was fourteen and so friggin' cute..." Kai smiled wistfully.

"How did it happen?"

They arrived at Myrtle Beach in South Carolina for their annual vacation. Kai immediately made a beeline for the beach. She wanted a tan and to get away from her parents. She took her brand new portable CD player and her favorite CD, Pearl Jam's Ten. *She had her headphones plugged firmly in, and didn't bother to look around her.*

People always looked at her; she was unusually tall for a girl, and with her dark hair and eyes, everyone always seemed to expect her to be foreign and not speak English. She'd been mistaken for Hispanic, Italian, Greek, even Middle Eastern; her actual ethnicity was never identified—mostly Asian with a touch of American Indian, which lent her skin its color that darkened easily in the sun.

She also spoke perfect English—better than most kids her age, since her father insisted on perfection in all things, including her speech and knowledge. It was easier for her to plug her headphones in and ignore everyone. Better to be thought a foreigner and therefore rude than have to deal with people.

At the shore, she sat down with her knees up to her chest, draping her arms over them. She stared out at the ocean for a long few minutes, then lay back on the sand, closing her eyes. She had no idea how long she'd been there when suddenly a shadow crossed her vision, blocking out the sun.

Opening her eyes, she looked up at the person standing above her, and was surprised to note that it was a girl—a blonde wearing cut-off shorts and a bikini top, staring down at her with a big smile on her face.

Kai reached up and removed one of her headphones. "Did you need something?" she asked, not sure whether the girl had said something to her.

"Yep. I need someone to come hang out with me at the pier," she said, her southern accent clear.

"Uhh…" Kai stammered in confusion.

"Ain't no one else interesting here."

"How do you know I'm interesting?" Kai asked as she levered herself up on her elbows.

"You look interesting," the girl said, her blue eyes sparkling.

"How?" Kai asked, expecting to hear the usual bullshit about being from a different country.

"Well, ain't you just as nervous as a long-tailed cat in a room full of rocking chairs…" the girl said. "I ain't gonna bite, ya know."

Kai looked back at her, not convinced, but she stood up just the same.

"I'm Scarlett," the girl said, putting out her hand. She smiled. "You know, like Gone With the Wind."

"Kai," Kai said simply, taking the girl's hand and shaking it once before letting it go.

"Kai?" Scarlett repeated, her southern accent sharp.

"Yes."

"That's a funny name," Scarlett said, her expression guileless.

"Like a name from a book written in 1936 is so very original," Kai replied evenly as she sat back down and put her headphones back in her ears.

She was surprised when Scarlett plopped down on the sand next to her, bumping her shoulder into Kai's as she did.

"How'd you know when that book was written?" Scarlett asked. "You read it or somethin'?"

Kai glanced at the girl, puzzled by her continued attention. "Yes, I read it last summer, along with the nine other novels on my summer reading list."

"What kind of fancy school do you go to that makes you read all that on summer vacation?"

"Emerson Prep," Kai said, her tone reflecting her mystified expression. "What difference does it make?"

"Ain't you big for your britches with your fancy school," Scarlett said, smiling all the same.

"You asked what school I go to that makes me read over summer vacation, I answered—why does that make me too big for my britches?"

The last thing she was was a braggart, and that was the last thing she'd allow herself to be called. The girl was seriously agitating, even if she did have really pretty blue eyes.

Scarlett laughed, shaking her head. "You are too much, Kai!" She put her hand on Kai's shoulder companionably and smiled engagingly. "Come with me to the pier."

"What's so interesting there?" Kai asked, not willing to be dragged off just anywhere by this girl.

"Me." Scarlett stood up again and grabbed Kai's hand, tugging her to her feet as well.

Kai noticed that Scarlett didn't drop her hand once she was up. She had to actually extricate it purposefully.

"Told ya I don't bite…" Scarlett said, winking at her as she started heading toward the pier.

Kai followed the girl, thinking she was probably just wasting her time, but she figured it was something to do. There was still plenty of time in the day to get a tan. When they reached the pier, Scarlett got her to wade out into the water by the pilings and showed her where a turtle was caught in a net wrapped around a piling farther out into the ocean.

"We have to do something," Kai said.

"How?" Scarlett asked. "It's too far out."

Kai reached into the pocket of her cargo shorts and pulled out her military-style Spyderco knife, unfolding it and putting it between her teeth as she started to wade further out.

"What are you doin'?" Scarlett called, suddenly sounding worried.

Kai didn't answer; she was too busy focusing on not getting slammed into a piling with the next wave coming in. She could see that the turtle was struggling desperately, and she was hoping it wouldn't hurt itself so badly it wouldn't survive even if she freed it. It did occur to her that she could drown in the process of trying to save the animal, but she felt like Mother Nature would be on her side.

She had to swim to reach the piling the turtle was caught up on. She managed to slice her leg on a barnacle on the post as she tried to hold on with her legs while working at cutting the net free.

"Hold on, little guy," she said. "Just hold on..."

A wave smacked her right in the face and she swallowed seawater, sputtering and coughing. Still she held on to the piling as best she could with her long legs and continued to work at the net. A few minutes and several cuts on her legs later, the turtle was free and swimming out with the tide.

Kai smiled even as Scarlett cheered from the shore. Putting the knife back between her teeth, Kai turned her head and was surprised to see a shark an arm's length away. Apparently Scarlett saw it at the same time because she screamed her name. Kai could tell the shark was looking at her. She reached up and took the Spyderco out of her mouth, holding it in her right hand.

"Hi," Kai said to the shark. "I'd appreciate it if you didn't eat me." She grinned, thinking if she was about to get bitten by a shark, there was no sense in going down without a fight.

She would not, however, attack him first. It wasn't in her to kill or hurt a living thing just because she could. The shark swished his tail slowly, maintaining his position near her but not coming any closer. Kai couldn't help but be fascinated by the encounter; if she hadn't been *afraid she'd lose a finger or two or five, she'd have put her hand out to touch the fish's hide.*

Finally the shark swam off and Kai grinned. She put her knife back between her teeth, not wanting to take the chance of losing one of her prized possessions. She headed back toward the shore, and as she walked up on the sand, Scarlett was shaking her head at her.

"Did you talk to that shark?"

Kai lay down on her back, trying to catch her breath, nodding in response to Scarlett's question.

"Are you crazy?" Scarlett said, sitting down on the sand next to her.

"Not that I'm aware of." Kai grinned, turning her head to look up at Scarlett.

"What did you say to the shark?" Scarlett asked, her blue eyes sparkling with humor.

"I told him I would appreciate it if he didn't eat me."

"And he listened. Fancy that."

"Guess so," Kai said, still breathing heavily.

"And you saved the turtle."

Kai nodded, closing her eyes.

"You're a hero," Scarlett said, grinning.

"To a turtle."

Kai suddenly felt Scarlett's hair on her face and opened her eyes; she found herself staring up into Scarlett's blue eyes.

"To me too," Scarlett said softly, then pressed her lips to Kai's.

Kai was surprised at first, but quickly felt her body responding to the soft pressure of Scarlett's lips on hers. She reached up to touch Scarlett's face as their lips parted, and Scarlett looked down at Kai, her eyes searching. Kai knew she was looking to see if what was happening was okay. To show her it was, she moved her head to kiss her. Scarlett sighed softly and pressed closer.

"I'm getting you wet," Kai said at one point, because Scarlett was half lying on her by that time.

"Yes, you are, sugar," Scarlett said. "Touch me."

Kai did as she bade. "Yes, just like that..." Scarlett said, her voice a low moan against Kai's lips.

Kai felt herself getting excited by the sheer insanity of what they were doing. They were out in the open, and even though it was very quiet on the beach, it didn't mean they couldn't be caught.

The continued to touch until they were both completely satisfied. All the while Kai was sure they'd get caught.

Afterward Kai lay panting, her face pressed against Scarlett's shoulder. "That was..." she began, but she couldn't think of the appropriate words to express how incredible the feeling had been.

"Yes, it was," Scarlett agreed, grinning.

"This isn't your first time, is it?"

"No." Scarlett shook her head, smiling softly.

"Is that why you talked to me?"

Scarlett looked back at her for a long moment, then smiled again. "I talked to you because I think you're very different—you're a butterfly in a sea of June bugs."

"Do I look strange?" Kai asked, her true insecurity coming to bear.

"You look butch."

"Butch?"

"Yeah. You have a little bit of a masculine look to you—it's neat."

Kai considered the thought. She'd always been referred to as a tomboy because she didn't wear makeup or dresses like other girls did. "Butch," she repeated, testing out the phrase.

Scarlett nodded, then smiled. "Definitely butch."

"Wow… So she's the one that told you that you were butch?" Cassiana asked when Kai had finished the story, just as she turned onto her street in Brentwood.

"Yep."

"Very cool," Cassiana said, smiling. "And holy shit—you live around here?"

"Language…"

Cassiana sighed. "What do you do for a living again?"

Kai grinned. "Well, a few things at this point, but mostly I'm a personal trainer."

"Like helping fat people get skinny?"

Kai chuckled. "Or helping people like Remington LaRoché get ready for a fight."

"You know Remington LaRoché?" Cassiana asked, her expression agog.

"I know a few famous people."

"Like who?"

"Xandy Blue, who"—Kai pointed to a house as they passed it—"lives right there."

"No lie?" Cassiana said, craning her neck to look at the house.

"No lie. And I know Wynter Kincade too."

"Well, yeah, she's like dating Remington LaRoché, isn't she?"

"Yes, she is," Kai said, nodding.

"Will I get to meet them?" Cassiana asked as Kai steered around the curve and reached for the remote for her garage door.

Kai grinned. "Probably."

"O… M… G!" Cassiana exclaimed as the garage door opened at the top of the drive to Kai's house. "This is yours?"

Kai nodded.

"Is that a Navigator?" Cassiana asked, seeing the large black SUV in the garage.

"Yeah. I use it for the boys."

"The what?"

Cassiana found out a couple of minutes later when they walked into the house. Two very large dogs came running around the curve of the entryway.

"Hold!" Kai commanded, even as she turned off the alarm to the house. "Sit!"

Both dogs halted immediately and their butts hit the floor at the second command.

Cassiana stared in fascination; she'd never owned a dog before. One was large pit bull with a massive head; the other dog was larger than the first and had the oddest coloring Cassiana had ever seen. His body was beige, but there was darker hair around his ears and his muzzle had dark spots on it. His eyes were almost white, they were such a light blue.

"That's Digger," Kai said, pointing to the dog with the light eyes. "And that's Chip."

"Chip?"

"For the chip on his shoulder when I rescued him from the shelter," Kai said, grinning.

"And Digger?"

"From the hole he dug in my arm the first time we met." She held out her right arm, showing Cassiana the scar on the inside of her forearm.

"Ouch," Cassiana said.

"Yeah. We've forgiven each other since then," Kai said, winking at Digger.

"What kind of dog is he?"

"He's an Afghan Shepherd, or Kuchi—they're herding dogs in Afghanistan."

"Can I just…" Cassiana started to say as she stepped toward the dogs.

"Wait," Kai said calmly, gently putting her hand on Cassiana's shoulder. "You have to approach a dog differently than you would a person. It's actually very poor dog behavior to approach a dog head on—it's a challenge to them."

"Okay," Cassiana said, her eyes slightly wide.

"Now, these two are well trained, but even the best-trained dog is still a little bit wild at heart, so you never know, and it's always better to be safe. So, what you do is turn to the side." Kai demonstrated. "And hold your hand out to the dogs from the side, so they can sniff you."

Cassiana did as she was told, putting her hand out to Digger first. Digger sniffed her fingers and licked them. Cassiana laughed.

"Now, before you approach him, since he's with another dog, you need to make sure the other dog is okay with you too," Kai said. "So do the same thing."

Cassiana did, and Chip sniffed her, putting his nose under her hand and pushing his head against it.

"What does that mean?" Cassiana asked.

"It means 'scratch my head, it itches,'" Kai said, grinning. She stepped toward the dogs and went down to one knee "Okay," she told them, and they both converged on her with licks and tail wags.

"Now you just approached them directly—why's that okay?" Cassiana asked. There was no attitude in her voice—it was obvious she was curious.

"Because I'm the leader of their pack," Kai said as Digger licked her face again.

"Pack?"

"Dogs travel in packs, like wolves. That's what they want most in life—to be part of a pack. Digger, Chip, and I are our own pack."

"Can I be part of your pack?" Cassiana asked as she petted Digger. He rubbed his head against her leg.

"Looks like you already are," Kai said, smiling.

After a tour of the house, Kai showed Cassiana the bedroom where she could put what little stuff she'd brought with her.

"This place is amazing, Kai," Cassiana said, gesturing around her.

"Wait till you see the view in the morning in the backyard—it's why I paid a fortune for it," Kai said. "I'm going to go take a shower and change. Make yourself at home, okay?"

"Okay." Cassiana smiled. "Thank you, Kai," she said, reaching out to hug her half-sister. "Thank you for being so awesome."

Kai hugged Cassiana fondly, kissing the top of her head. "You're my little sister—what else am I gonna do?"

Cassiana squeezed Kai extra tight for that, happy that she thought of her that way.

Twenty minutes later Kai emerged from the master bathroom, dressed in her usual sleeping attire for the winter—a white tank top and black yoga pants that hugged her slim hips and outlined her thighs then belled at the calves.

"Now there's a sight…" Kathy said from the bed where she was lounging.

"What the fuck are you doing in here?" Kai snapped in surprise.

"Your sister, is it? She let me in," Kathy said, smiling smugly.

"Well, you can let yourself out." Kai put her hands up on the door frame between the master bath and the bedroom.

"I don't know why we have to play this game, Kai," Kathy said as she got off the bed, her blue eyes sparkling.

"It's not a game, Kat," Kai said, her lips twitching at the fact that Kathy was walking toward her. "You need to leave."

"I'm not leaving. Not until you let me fuck you…" Kai reached out to touch Kai's stomach.

Kai stepped back. "That's not going to happen."

Kathy laughed sarcastically. "Really? When you're afraid to even let me touch you?"

"Does it occur to you that maybe I don't want you to touch me?"

"Not really, no."

Her tone was so casual that Kai was lulled for a moment, so much so that she wasn't expecting Kathy to step forward, so close that Kai couldn't have avoided her without literally leaping back. Kathy's hand was immediately sliding up under Kai's tank top, moving over her abdomen seductively. Kai's body lit up like a Christmas tree, making her crave what she knew Kathy could supply—mind-blowing orgasms.

She had no true idea how or why the other woman had such an incredible hold on her sexually, but the fact was she did. And in capturing Kai's libido so completely, Kathy had also captured her heart, and then thrown it away time and time again.

As Kathy reached up to slide her other hand around Kai's neck, intent on pulling her head down to kiss her, the way she always closed the deal, Kai pulled her head back and took a long step away, holding up her hands when Kathy tried to follow.

"Don't!" Kai practically yelled.

Kathy stopped, in sheer reaction to the vehemence in Kai's voice. A sudden scratching and canine whining could be heard at Kai's closed bedroom door. The door started shaking with the force of the two dogs throwing themselves against it in an effort to get to their master. Kai knew they'd heard the warning in her raised voice, and they were responding to it.

"Kai?" Cassiana queried from the other side of the door. "Should I let them in?"

"Yes," Kai said, her eyes on Kathy; she knew she was not the least bit fond of dogs.

Kathy's eyes widened as the door opened and the dogs bounded in, immediately moving to Kai's side, taking up flanking positions next to her in the bathroom hallway. Kai couldn't help but grin as the boys stood looking up at her in concern.

"Make them sit, Kai," Kathy said, her nervousness obvious.

Kai curled her lip in derision. "You make them sit," she said disdainfully.

"You know I can't." Kathy backed up a step as the boys responded to her nervousness and stepped toward her. "Kai!"

"Hold," Kai said, and both dogs stopped their forward movement.

"Get them out of here," Kathy said authoritatively.

"They live here—you don't," Kai said. "So just turn around and leave, or I'll give them the command to attack."

"You wouldn't do that," Kathy said, her tone a little less sure.

"Wanna bet?" Kai asked, her dark eyes sparkling maliciously.

"Okay, I'll leave," Kathy said, her expression far from defeated. "But when I get to you—and I will get to you, Kai—you're going to beg me to fuck you, and you're going to wish to hell you hadn't played games with me."

Kai nodded, far from worried. Kathy backed up to the door as Kai walked forward and gave the dogs the hand command to heel. Each dog took up a side as Kai followed Kathy out to the front door and closed it behind her. Kai turned to put her back to the door, banging her head against the hard wood a few times, making the intricate stained-glass pieces artistically set within it rattle.

"Who was that?" Cassiana asked, walking into the foyer and seeing what Kai was doing. "And why are you banging your head like that?"

Kai looked over at her sister. "That was my ex, and do not ever let her in this house again, okay?"

"The dogs went nuts when you yelled."

"Yeah, they heard the tension in my voice and responded to it."

Cassiana grinned. "Pretty cool."

"Yeah, it is," Kai said, grinning too. "I'm headed to bed. Good night." She went over to hug Cassiana and kiss the top of her head.

"Good night," Cassiana said, hugging her back.

Chapter 2

When Cassiana woke the next morning, she looked around her room and smiled. The bright California sun was shining through the windows. The room itself was beautiful with its sage green walls and bright white crown molding and framed windows. The happiest thing of all was that she was there with her half-sister, the one person she'd come to rely on over the last two years to make her feel better.

She remembered well the first email she'd sent to Kai; she had queried cautiously if it was okay to write to her there in California. She still had Kai's response. It had said simply:

You are the daughter of my father, and therefore my family. Of course you can write me. I would love to get to know you. ~Kai~

Cassiana had been so happy to receive that email. It meant that at least someone in the Temple family didn't consider her some kind of trespasser in their lives. The fact was, she'd had no say in the matter. Her mother, who'd always been somewhat distant with her, had handed her over to the Temples and taken off on her next assignment in Turkey. At first Cassiana had been happy, not having to go to yet another foreign country where people treated her like she was strange. Her entire high school career had been achieved online. At least in Washington DC she would get to go to a regular high school with other American kids. It had been heaven at first, but she'd quickly felt stifled by the slower pace of a regular brick-and-mortar school. When she asked her father if she could switch back to online school, he'd nodded without any real consideration. It had been Kai who'd talked to her about it in a chat session.

Cassie: Asked to go back to online HS today

Kai: Why?

Cassie: This school is too slow for me!

Kai: Okay, but you said you liked interacting with other students.

Cassie: I do, but my God it's going to take a thousand years just to get through algebra!

Kai: LOL too smart for your own good

Cassie: You think so?

Kai: Oh I know so, I had the same problem, that's why they switched me to Emerson

Prep

Cassie: What's that?

Kai: It's a private high school. Didn't they give you that option?

Cassie: Nope, never mentioned it.

The cursor for the chat session had blinked more than a few times before Kai answered her. Cassiana had no way of knowing that Kai had been cursing their father for not giving this girl the same benefits she'd been given. Whether he liked it or not, the girl was his blood, and she should be given every advantage of that. Kai didn't like that Marou Temple was treating Cassiana as if she weren't valuable to him. She knew that feeling well; he'd always treated her the same way. She wasn't a boy, so she wasn't what he'd wanted.

Kai: Ask Dad about it.

Cassie: Kai, I don't want to be a pain.

Kai: You want a good education, Cassie, trust me on that. With a good education you can do anything you want in life.

Cassie: Okay

Kai: Will you ask, or do I need to call our father?

Cassiana had smiled at that. Kai Marou Temple wasn't the kind of person to sit back and wait, or take whatever someone was willing to give her.

Cassie: Is Emerson where you learned to be so brave?

Kai: LOL No, I learned that later.

Cassie: I hope it's genetic!

Kai: I will talk to our father if you don't want to.

Cassie: I will ask them about it.

Kai: Them?

Cassie: You know, our father and your mother

Kai: Don't bother including my mother, she doesn't get to make decisions.

Cassie: That's harsh

Kai: That's reality, Cass. Just talk to our father and let me know what he says.

Cassie: Okay I will. Thanks!

Cassiana talked to their father that night, and Marou had been non-committal about the option. Later he had decided that Cassiana should just continue with online classes to finish her high school degree. It had cemented in Cassiana's mind the idea that she wasn't even important enough to her father to receive a good education. Kai had been furious. It had been the first of many fights Kai had had with him over Cassiana.

Cassiana pulled on her sweatshirt and jeans and walked out of the bedroom. Standing in the long galley kitchen, she looked out the kitchen window at the view of the canyon and the hills surrounding the house. She heard barking outside and realized Kai must actually be awake and outside. It was only six in the morning on a Saturday—the woman woke up that early?

As Cassiana walked toward the back door, she heard music playing and saw Kai sitting in one of the patio chairs, her long legs bent at the knees and in a wide stance. She was leaning forward with her elbows on her knees, her head down. She had a cigarette in one hand, the smoke curling from the tip. Watching her, Cassiana could see she was singing along to the music. Cassiana focused on the words of the song. It was Adele's "Rolling in the Deep." Kai sang the bridge and chorus with relish, and Cassiana was sure that she was thinking of Kathy. The lyrics talked about how the other person had left her scarred, and how she'd had her heart played with mercilessly.

"Was she that bad?" Cassiana asked as she walked out the back door.

Kai turned her head, looking at her half-sister. "Yeah," she said, the emotions clear on her face.

"You smoke?" Cassiana asked, sitting in the chair next to Kai's.

Kai leaned back, taking a drag on the cigarette and blowing the smoke out a few long moments later. "Only when I'm stressed," she said, setting the cigarette aside.

"What did she do to you?"

Kai shook her head. "Long story. But suffice it to say that she really did a number on me."

Cassiana nodded, not liking that anyone had hurt her sister.

"You're Temple?" asked the colonel sitting behind her desk, surveying this lieutenant colonel under her new command.

"Yes, ma'am," Kai responded, keeping her eyes focused straight ahead.

"Didn't know I had a female lieutenant colonel under my command," Kathy Binder said, her blue eyes scanning Kai's uniform and the eagle on her collar. "It says here you've got nine years in?"

"Yes, ma'am."

"At ease, Temple," Kathy said, waving her hand airily.

Kai assumed a more relaxed position but continued to stare straight ahead, even when the new colonel stood up and walked around to sit on her desk in front of her.

"How'd you make lieutenant colonel inside of nine years, Temple?" Kathy asked derisively. "You fuck your way there?"

Kai's gaze flickered as her eyes narrowed ever so slightly. "No, ma'am."

"But it pisses you off that I think you did," Kathy said, seeing the slight change in Kai's attitude.

Kai inclined her head slightly.

"I've put fifteen years in to make colonel," Kathy said, "and I did

fuck someone to get here. She was worth every second, but…" She let her voice trail off as Kai's eyes widened at such confidence being shared so casually.

Don't Ask, Don't Tell was very firmly in place in the military, and the idea of her commanding officer flat out telling her that she had had sex with a woman to get her position was insane.

"Is that shock or excitement, Temple?" Kathy asked, moving to stand very close to Kai, staring up at her.

Kai dropped her dark eyes to look down at Kathy. "Shock, ma'am."

"Why? Because you heard I was married to a man? Or because I just told you I fucked a woman?"

Kai didn't respond. Instead she refocused her eyes on a point on the wall behind Kathy.

Kathy started to grin. She knew a butch lesbian when she set eyes on one, and this one was incredibly hot. She hadn't been lying when she said she'd fucked someone to get her position. She had—she'd even married the son of a bitch to cement the deal. She'd also fucked women, and she'd found she liked that much better. It was a new challenge, and Kathy loved a challenge.

She'd read Kai Temple's file, and it was indeed impressive. The picture of the woman had made her hot, so she'd known she needed to meet with her and see if she could get to her. She could see now that Kai was definitely a Marine through and through. So she decided that the very appropriate Kai Temple was her new mission; it would make this time in the desert worthwhile. One way or the other, she'd get the very "Marine's Marine"—as Kai had been referred to by her previous commander—to bend her over this very desk and fuck her. Just the idea of it had Kathy dismissing Kai and going into her private bathroom to take care of that ache, thinking of her the entire time.

"So are you interested in meeting some of my friends?" Kai asked when the silence had stretched too long.

Cassiana smiled. "Um, sure."

"I need to go down to the gym I'm looking into buying into, and a lot of the people I hang out with these days are usually there." She winked at Cassiana. "You can meet Remington LaRoché in person."

"That would be awesome!"

"Okay, be ready to leave here in about an hour and a half," Kai said, getting up and stretching.

Cassiana stared up at her big sister and couldn't help but admire the way she looked. There was something very powerful and exotic about Kai Marou Temple. She was someone people noticed wherever she went.

Finley was busy trying to keep up with Natalia's latest routine when movement to her right caught her eye. She was used to all the "bois" standing off to the side near the half-wall of the studio to watch their wives or girlfriends dance. Those were the ones that hadn't joined Remington's group doing the MMA fight-style training in the studio's other room. Finley glanced over and saw the dark-haired, strongly built woman she'd seen at The Club the last time Memphis had DJed. It had been a month since then.

She watched as the woman walked over to Dakota, extending her hand and introducing a young girl to her. The woman looked over to the dance floor then, her eyes searching; they found Jazmine, who was dancing just in front of Finley. A smile lit the woman's face and Finley saw Jazmine wave to her. The woman had a killer smile, Finley noted. She jumped when Natalia walked past her, swatting her playfully on the ass to tell her to pay attention.

Finley glanced back at the dark-haired woman and noted that she was now looking at her with a grin on her lips. Their stares connected for a second, and the woman rolled her eyes and shook her head. Finley laughed. Natalia was well known for her feisty little attitude, and apparently the dark-haired stranger had seen the swat she'd received and found it funny too.

"Cass, this is Dakota," Kai said, nodding at Dakota as they shook hands. "Dakota, this is my little sister, Cassiana. Dakota, her girl Jazmine, Natalia—the instructor over there—and her girl, Raine, own the building."

Dakota looked surprised even as she extended her hand to Cassiana, who took it, smiling.

"I didn't know you had a sister," Dakota said to Kai.

"Well, she's usually in DC with our father and my mother," Kai said, grinning as Remington and Quinn walked up.

"Sa a se ki?" Remington asked, looking at Cassiana.

"My sister," Kai said, having understood Remington's Creole. "She asked who you are," she told Cassiana, seeing her sister's blank look. "Remi forgets that not everyone speaks Creole."

"If she had her way, we all would," Quinn said, extending her hand to Cassiana. "I'm Quinn."

Cassiana's eyes widened. She'd seen the news stories on Quinn and Xandy a couple of years before, when Quinn had lifted part of a roof up off Xandy's baby cousin. She was amazed she was meeting these people.

"It's really great to meet you," she said. "Remington, I saw that fight with Akasha Salt—you were really amazing."

Remington inclined her head. "Mèsi."

"That means *thank you*," Cassiana said, smiling. "Creole is a lot like French, isn't it?"

Remington looked impressed. "It has its basis in French, yes."

Cassiana bit her lip, smiling.

Some of the others in the group walked over then, having seen Kai.

"Cass, this is Jet," Kai said, pointing to a woman with black hair and really beautiful light blue eyes; she was attractive in a very hot butch way.

Cassiana could only nod, too dazzled by Jet's looks to form an actual sentence.

"And this is Cody," Kai said, pointing to another butch girl who had white-blonde hair.

Cody was cute too, Cassiana thought—they sure didn't make ugly lesbians in Los Angeles! "Hi," she said, smiling shyly.

"And this is Jericho." Kai pointed to a woman about an inch taller than Kai with long black hair and bright blue eyes. She had a very exotic look, different than Kai's, but she was definitely a very hot-looking butch too.

"Jericho is a very cool name," Cassiana said. "Where are you from?"

"Iran," Jericho said, her pronunciation very clearly the proper one.

"Iran," Cassiana repeated, doing her best to get the intonation. "Is that the right way to say it?"

Jericho smiled. "It is."

"So most people say it wrong?"

"They do," Jericho said, nodding.

Cassiana smiled. "Rude."

Jericho chuckled; it was a deep, rumbling sound. Cassiana decided she liked her right away.

"Jericho is the director for the Division of Law Enforcement at the Department of Justice. And someone I have a meeting with this week," Kai said, grinning.

"For what?" Cassiana asked.

Kai waggled her eyebrows. "Oh, some crazy idea I have."

"Is this the idea about the dogs?" Cody asked, having heard about it from the law enforcement liaison Kai had been with a month before when the Rottweiler had gotten loose.

"Yeah," Kai said.

Cody nodded, looking happy, and glanced at Jericho. "It's a really good idea."

"Well, we'll see, won't we?" Jericho said, smiling.

"Cass, this is Rayden," Kai said then, gesturing to another tall woman with long black hair and features that very definitely looked American Indian.

"Are you Native American?" Cassiana asked.

"I am," Rayden said with a grin. "I'm Cherokee."

"Wow," Cassiana said, widening her eyes. "That's really cool. I'm so many things I don't even know what all..." She let her voice trail off as she shook her head.

"And this is Sebastian and Kashena Windwalker-Marshal—she's American Indian too," Kai said, smiling at a blonde woman with deep blue eyes.

"I'm only half," Kashena said. "But my wife—Sierra, out there at the end in the pink—is full blood."

"And I'm not Indian at all," Sebastian said with a grin, his stormy green eyes twinkling with humor.

Cassiana laughed.

"And that's Memphis over there," Kai said, and glanced at Remington. "What's she doing?"

"Grabbing Nat's playlist," Remington said. "Nat wants her to do some mixes for her, to 'spice things up.'" She said the last with air quotes.

Kai's eyes trailed out to the floor where the women were currently doing a routine that involved a lot of rather seductive hip movements. "Things need to be spicier?"

"I think Nat's trying to kill us bois," Jet said, grinning.

"Good possibility," Cody said.

"Of it killing us, or of that being what she's trying to do?" Quinn asked.

"Both," Cody said with an engaging smile.

"I think it's her way of telling us to stop watching and get to work," Tyler said from behind the group.

"Hey, Tyler," Kai said, nodding to the other woman. "You on this morning?" She'd noted that Tyler was wearing her Air Force BDUs.

"Just getting off, actually," Tyler said, rolling her eyes. "They're makin' me nuts with this election bullshit."

"It's affecting you guys?" Rayden asked.

"Yeah, the whole security issue for LAX, they've got us manning areas. It's a nightmare, trust me."

"Sorry," Kai said, shaking her head. "Tyler, this is my sister, Cassiana."

"Good to meet you," Tyler said, smiling.

"You're in the Air Force?" Cassiana asked.

"Yeah."

"And a major," Kai said, recognizing the gold oak leaf on Tyler's collar. "That's new, isn't it?"

"Yeah." Tyler grinned. "They're worried I'll quit."

"Probably 'cause you threatened to last year," Jet pointed out.

"True," Tyler said, her blue eyes sparkling.

"You were going to quit?" Jericho asked, sounding surprised.

"When I just about lost Shenin because I wasn't able to be here in LA, yeah," Tyler said, looking emotional.

Jet clapped her hand on Tyler's shoulder. It had been a rough time for all for them. Shenin, Tyler's wife, had tried to kill herself, and Jet had almost been killed in a helicopter accident.

Cassiana watched the two, glancing at Kai a couple of times. She noticed that Kai looked pained. She was ever empathetic with how the military could ruin relationships.

When the class ended, Jazmine and Natalia came over while the bois said their quick goodbyes and went to claim their girls.

"She hasn't had any time to actually look at the space," Dakota told Jazmine and Natalia.

"I'm looking now," Kai said, her eyes scanning the room.

"And?" Dakota asked, her eyes sparkling.

Kai nodded. "I like it. I'd want some changes…"

"I can make any change you want," Dakota said. "We can just amortize it with your lease."

"Yeah, about that…" Kai said. "What would you say to me paying for any changes and investing with you in this place?"

Dakota and Jazmine glanced at each other, then over at Natalia.

"How far in are you and Raine?" Kai asked.

"Fifty thousand dollars," Natalia said, her dark eyes narrowing as she tried to divine what Kai was doing.

Kai nodded, then looked back to Dakota and Jazmine. "And you two?"

"More—a lot more," Dakota said, grinning.

"So could two hundred K buy me in?"

Dakota, Jazmine, Natalia, and Cassiana all looked stunned.

Finally Dakota nodded. "If you want to go that deep, anywhere from fifty thousand to the two hundred would be fine too."

"I'll go the two hundred. I'd like to start the adjustments sooner rather than later—I can give you fifty K in cash this week, and then the rest when we've finished and have agreed to a lease?"

"There wouldn't be a lease," Dakota said. "You'd just share in the profit—what we'll agree to is the percentage."

Kai grinned. "Okay."

****

Finley looked across at the brunette she was seeing currently. She had lovely blue eyes and an adorable shape, and she was twenty years old. Finley had met her at The Club, a place she'd been frequenting since seeing one extremely attractive dark-haired butch. The good-looking butch hadn't been back in, but the brunette was a decent find.

"Can we get the Osetra caviar?" Ginny asked, her eyes wide as she twirled a lock of her hair.

"Why do you want caviar?" Finley asked.

"Isn't it supposed to be good?"

"Do you even know what it is?"

"Um..." Ginny stammered.

"It's fish eggs."

Ginny visibly paled.

"Yeah, so you might want to stick with something you actually recognize," Finley said, winking at the girl.

Ginny simply giggled and opted for a fifty-dollar lobster salad.

Finley was used to it. They figured she was a doctor so she had to be rich; that's why someone like Ginny would want to order $160 caviar to "try" it. Her condominium only served to reinforce their thinking. They had no way of knowing that her mother had paid for two-thirds of the place. It wasn't to say that she didn't make decent money, but it was far less than the rich plastic surgeons people saw on TV. She knew private practice was probably the more lucrative way to go—she could train in plastic surgery or any of the other disciplines—but she liked working in the trauma unit. She felt like she was making a difference.

During dinner Finley was regaled with Ginny's shopping trip that afternoon. There were a lot of "OMG"s and "OMFG"s and even some "LOL"ing—at which Finley found herself wanting to explain to the child that she could actually just laugh out loud, but she didn't really think it would help.

"So what did you say to the clerk who'd leveled such a baseless accusation?" Finley asked.

"I... huh?" Ginny said with the blankest look Finley had seen in a while.

"Sorry," Finley muttered, thinking, *What was I thinking, using adults' words on you?* "I meant, what did you say to the guy who thought you stole the lipstick?"

Ginny laughed. "Oh, I just told him to KMA and walked out of the store."

Finley looked back at the girl for a long moment. Ginny had already told her that the guy was old—"like, at least fifty"—so she was fairly sure Ginny's put down had escaped him. Telling him to "kiss my ass" in an acronym that was mostly known to young people was only a way to prove his point, not hers. But why bother explaining that? She gave a fairly hollow laugh, which to Ginny meant she was hilarious.

Later, still in The Club, Finley kept an eye open for the dark-haired butch, but she wasn't sure why. She didn't date butch women—never had, and never planned to start. It was like the woman was some kind of fascination for her, probably because she'd only ever seen her twice. She remembered well the nasty things the blond woman had said to her and how the dark-haired butch had responded—or failed to respond—in the blonde's presence. It hadn't jibed in her head. The dark-haired butch seemed much more the dominant type than the submissive, although the blonde had stated that she was her "superior." Maybe it was literally a domme/femme relationship.

Regardless, Finley wanted to at least have the chance to admire the woman again. She'd almost asked Remington about her friend a few times, but knew that would just get around too quickly. Although she'd been accepted as part of the group after making the house call to check Memphis' wounds and stitch her up, Finley didn't trade on it or expect anything.

There were thirty-two people in the group—thirty-one women and one man—not that they referred to themselves as "the group" in any kind of official way. And not that they were ever all at The Club at the same time, except for special occasions, like the night she'd seen the dark-haired butch for the first time at Memphis' special spin for her friends who'd helped her and for Minnie, the owner. But they were definitely a force to be reckoned with.

Finley found that out later that night. She'd gone down to the bathroom and was coming back up the stairs when a drunk but bigger femme came barreling down them. Finley did her best to flatten herself against the wall to avoid contact, but it didn't work and down the two of them went. Fortunately it was only five steps, but it stunned Finley for a minute, and suddenly the other woman was hurtling insults at her for "tripping" her. Finley got to her feet, unwilling to literally lie down and take the woman's screaming and cussing.

Natalia, who'd been on her way to the bathroom and had seen what happened, ran to grab Remington and Quinn. They were closest, since they were keeping an eye on their girls as well as others in the group.

"Remi, Quinn!" Natalia yelled at the top of her lungs.

Within a minute Remington was hurrying down the stairs and moving between the femme and Finley, who had just stepped back as the other woman raised her fist to hit her.

"I don't think you're going to be doing that," Remington said, her hazel eyes narrowed at the woman.

"Don't fucking tell me what I'm gonna do and not gonna do, bitch," the dark-haired woman snapped back.

Quinn, who'd move in behind Remington and was putting Finley's arm around her neck to help her up the stairs, looked over at the young femme.

"I don't think I'd cuss at Remi if I were you either, love," Quinn said, her Irish accent clear.

"Who the fuck are you two? Her bodyguards or what?" the woman said, laughing. She clearly thought she was hilarious.

Remington and Quinn exchanged a look, both knowing that the girl was more drunk than stupid. Remington gave Quinn an upward lift of her head to tell her to take Finley upstairs. The femme, however, wasn't having that.

"Hey! We weren't done!" she said, stepping past Remington to grab at Finley's arm.

Remington's vice-like hand encircled the woman's wrist gently but firmly. "Don't touch her."

"This is between me and her." The woman tried to yank her hand out of Remington's grip. "Let me go, damnit!" she screamed, looking up at the rest of the crowd on the stairs—people she'd just tried to blow past to get to the bathroom first, and also some who actually knew Remington's and Quinn's reputations and that this woman was just too drunk for her own good.

Remington pulled the young femme closer to her, leaning down. "Calm down and I will let you go. But be warned, if you try and go after my friend again, I won't have any trouble stopping you."

"You'd think she was your lover or something," the femme snapped, though a little less sharply now as her idiotic behavior seemed to be heading beyond even her own boundaries of smart.

"My lover is upstairs with the rest of my friends, but I take the protection of women quite seriously, I assure you," Remington said.

"Well, you're manhandling me just fine. That doesn't seem to bother you!"

"Because Finley didn't start this—you did with her, because you were embarrassed that you fell down some stairs."

"She tripped me!"

"Our friend who was standing in line saw what happened," Remington said. "So you can let that lie go right now. Finley is a doctor—she would never deliberately hurt someone who she'd likely see in her ER a half hour later."

The femme was done then, realizing that really she had just been embarrassed—because fat girls always fall down, right? She'd latched onto Finley because she was so pretty and skinny...

Suddenly she had tears running down her cheeks. She knew it was the alcohol and the fact that she'd peed herself when she'd fallen and that people would make fun of her when they smelled it. She felt her wrist being let go, and glanced up at the strong woman with cornrowed hair and light-colored eyes.

"I'm sorry," she said simply, crying harder.

She was stunned when she felt arms encircle her in a hug. It was the same woman that had been holding her wrist just moments before.

"Let me help you get out of here and get you a cab home, bebe," Remington said, having smelled the urine and guessed that the tears were more embarrassment and alcohol than actual hurt.

The young femme nodded miserably.

Remington carefully moved them up the stairs, keeping her body between the girl and the women standing in line for the bathroom so the smell would be less noticeable. At the top, she pulled out her phone, and keeping one arm around the girl, she used her other hand to unlock it and request an Uber pickup.

"I heard what happened—is Finley okay?" asked Minnie from the sidebar.

"She looked fine, but go check—she's with the group." Upon

seeing Minnie's narrowed eyes, Remington added, "It was an accident. We've got it handled, Minnie."

"If you say so, Remi..." Minnie said, trailing off to indicate to the girl that she was lucky Remington was handling this, and not her.

Remington nodded, and led the girl to the front of the club. Outside, she turned to her, taking her face gently in her hands. "Are you okay? Do you need to be seen by a doctor?"

"Like the one I just took down with me?" the girl said, crying again.

"What's your name?"

"Tammy," she replied, her head bent in embarrassment.

"Tammy, I'm Remi. Accidents do happen, and sometimes we let things get away from us. I think that's what happened tonight, right?"

Tammy nodded. "I'm so sorry. Please tell your friend that I'm sorry."

"I'll do that," Remington said as the Uber pulled up. She helped Tammy to the car.

"What's the address?" the driver asked.

"410 West Pico, but you need my credit card," Tammy said as Remington shut the cab door.

"Been paid for—just need the address," the driver said.

Tammy rolled down the window. "You didn't have to do that," she said to Remington.

"I want you to get home safe." Remington put her hand on Tammy's arm, which she was resting on the window frame. "Take care," she said, and stepped back with a grin.

It was something Tammy would never forget, the night a handsome butch took care of her even when she was in the wrong.

In the meantime, Quinn had taken Finley upstairs and over to the group, though not before Natalia and Raine had gotten to Quinn first. Fadiyah was called in from the patio where she was talking to Jet as her wife smoked.

"Guys, I'm fine, really," Finley said, embarrassed by the flurry of attention.

"That why you're limping?" Dakota asked.

"Well, I probably twisted my ankle a bit—high heels are not conducive to falling down stairs."

"Your arm is bleeding too," Fadiyah stated as she walked up. "Jet, can you please get Minnie's first aid kit?"

"Of course," Jet said with a nod, and jogged over to the bar.

"Please just have a seat, and be careful. That dress is lovely—I would hate for blood to ruin it," Fadiyah said, her voice so smooth Finley didn't realize she was being managed for a few moments.

Ginny had come rushing over when she saw Quinn helping Finley up the stairs. "My God, what happened?" she gasped, seeing blood on Finley's arm.

"I'm okay," Finley said.

Ginny didn't hear it, because she suddenly realized where she was. She was in the midst of the group, and everyone knew who they were. Her eyes darted from face to face as she mentally ticked off each of them. She couldn't miss Wynter Kincade or Xandy Blue, but she'd also recognized Quinn Kavanaugh right off the bat. The other women she'd seen but didn't know much about, including their names. Hell, it was part of the reason she was going out with the rich doctor, so she could meet the group that she knew Finley was friendly with.

Quinn and Xandy exchanged a look. Quinn shook her head slightly, indicating she didn't like this match at all. A grin twitched at Xandy's lips as she recognized Quinn's disapproval, finding it amusing that Quinn laid all of the blame for the matchmaking at her feet and rarely at her own. Xandy was always entertained by the way Quinn liked to see things.

Later, back at Finley's house, Ginny went on and on about the girls and how really cool they all were. Finley nodded, not for the first time in the twenty-minute gush session. The sex was expectedly mediocre that night, and not Finley's part in it. That was the problem with younger women—what they lacked in experience they should make up for in imagination and staying power. Score zero for zero for youth on this night.

****

"So you take dogs out of the shelter and train them?" asked Jericho—the director for the Division of Law Enforcement for the California Department of Justice, easily one of the most powerful women in law enforcement at that moment. Her feet were up on her desk as she leaned back in her chair, looking across at Kai.

Kai nodded. "Yes."

"And you'd charge how much to train them?"

"Five thousand dollars for each dog that passes a six-month qual," Kai said, her pose much less casual.

Jericho could easily see the ex-Marine in her, just as she could always see it in Kashena's stance. They even seemed to sit at attention. She nodded slowly, her expression calculating. "What's the cost of acquiring the dogs?"

"Nothing."

Jericho turned her head slightly, giving Kai a sidelong look "How much does a K9 normally cost?"

"I hear you can pick up a decently trained one for around twenty thousand," Kai murmured.

"So you're basically offering me four dogs for the price of one," Jericho mused. "Is that a financially sound strategy for you?"

Kai smiled mildly. "You leave that for me to worry about."

Jericho inclined her head. She knew this was a matter close to Kai's heart, but didn't want to take advantage of a friend. "So what do you see as the application for these dogs within DOJ?"

"The possibilities are endless," Kai said, spreading her long-fingered hands wide. "Obviously drug detection, but also chemical detections, like your labs group, or plastique, PTEN or RTX, weapons caches—that's what we used them for a lot in Afghanistan—or even body detection, live or dead."

"What about money?"

"Can they find money?"

"Yeah, obviously it'd have to be scented differently from the money in, say, my pocket or yours, but..."

"Well, yeah, if it's different... like fake?" Kai asked, picking up on Jericho's train of thought. "Yeah," she said with certainty when Jericho nodded.

Jericho got up, extending her hand to Kai, who also stood. "I'm definitely interested," she said. "I need to send it up to Midnight, and I guarantee she will want a demonstration. I know I want to see you work the dogs…" She let her voice trail off in her own enthusiasm. "Yeah, I suck as a client—too much open excitement," she said. "It's a great opportunity for us, and Midnight better approve it or I might get my own credit card out." She winked at Kai.

Kai laughed. "Then Zoey'll just kill you."

"Probably."

"Let's try this way first. I don't want to be responsible for breaking up a marriage—that'd get around…"

Jericho laughed outright at that, nodding. "Okay, throw together the proposal for Midnight, including your figures, and get it up to her. As soon as I hear back from her, I'll get ahold of you with some dates for a demo, okay?"

"Sounds good. Thanks, Jericho." Kai shook the other woman's hand, her eyes level with Jericho's even at her height of five foot nine, direct and sincere.

After Kai left, Jericho sat down at her desk and looked over the information Kai had given her. She shook her head slowly as a grin started on her lips. She was beginning to wonder if it was ever going to stop being Christmas at DOJ lately. With this resource she'd have air and ground coverage like never before and could maybe turn the tide on this war they were attempting to wage.

She turned to her computer and started typing, firing an email off to Midnight Chevalier.

****

Kai and Cassiana were just coming back from grocery shopping, Kai having bought more junk food than she'd purchased in many years. She'd already informed Cassiana that her eating was going to change, but she'd phase her off the junk food slowly so as not to send her young body into too much of a shock. She'd said that grinning.

They'd just gotten back in the Navigator when Kai's phone rang. She hit hands-free on the display as she backed out of the parking lot, even as she glanced at the display on her phone and grimaced.

"Hello," she said, keeping her tone mild.

"Kai," barked a man's voice.

Cassiana quickly recognized it as their father's, and winced at how much anger and accusation he'd managed to stuff into Kai's short name. "Dad, look, it's not Kai's fault," she began.

Kai put her hand out to touch Cassiana's, even as they both felt the tension on the phone line go up a couple of notches.

"Are you speaking to me, Cassiana McGinnt?" Marou Temple asked, very clearly emphasizing that she was not a Temple to him, nor that she had any right to take such liberties.

Cassiana blinked a couple of times at the impact of his words, and Kai's lips curled in anger at what he'd just done to the kid. It was one thing for him to have cut her to the quick like that over the years—she'd been raised by him and his family and their ways, but Cassiana hadn't. Naturally the mighty Marou Temple wasn't going to soften his ways for a girl.

"So talk to me, sir. What is it you need?" Kai snapped, not giving a damn about the sharpness in her voice.

"Kai, you must send Cassiana home right now."

"Let me guess, you got the boarding school all lined up?" Kai asked mildly, even as she saw Cassiana look over at her in sheer terror. Kai put her hand out to Cassiana and shook her head. She wondered how many languages she was being cursed in—he knew seven—for being a disrespectful child.

"You will do as you're told," Marou said, gritting it out between clenched teeth.

"Yeah…" Kai said. "Not gonna happen this time, sir, I'm sorry. She doesn't belong in military school. She wouldn't make it there."

"You were fine in military school."

Kai laughed, a mirthless sound. "How would you know?"

"Excuse me?"

"You wouldn't have known if I was alright in military school, sir, because you never checked. You just took the credit when I graduated with honors."

"What does this matter? You will send Cassiana home tonight."

"You gonna tell them she's gay too?" Kai asked, and waited for a full minute for an answer that didn't come. "You gonna do that to her too, sir? Make sure they know she's a dyke so they can try to beat it out of her until they break her? Or until they kill her?" The last was said with so much venom mixed with pain that it had Cassiana reaching both hands over to Kai to hold the arm closest to her.

To defend her, Kai was using every weapon in her arsenal, even if it hurt her and exposed her. Cassiana couldn't imagine not having this warrior at her side. She'd never have made it alone against their

71

father; she didn't have Kai's strength or confidence, and their father terrified her.

Marou Temple was a large man standing six feet two inches and weighing 220 pounds, most of which was muscle, with the dark, fierce looks of his Indian ancestors. He'd also inherited his Japanese ancestors' habit of abandoning their daughters. Fate had only given him girls, however, and he was about to lose both of them.

"I have another suggestion," Kai said into the silence.

It took Marou another full minute to muster a response. "What is it?"

"Let me take over custody." Kai glanced over at Cassiana and saw a smile of wonder bloom, but it was quickly quelled as Cassiana began to fear they would hear a booming "No."

"You are the reason this happened," Marou said conversationally.

Kai shook her head. "I know, I somehow managed to make someone I've never met in person gay. Hell, maybe it was the room, or… you know, they do say it's genetic…"

"Stop!" Marou commanded, even as Kai and Cassiana had to practically stuff their hands in their mouths to keep from laughing out loud.

"So what do you say, sir? Ready to stop being a dad?"

Again there was silence. Kai and Cassiana pulled up to the house as Marou answered. "It will be done," he said, as simply as if he were selling a car.

"Excellent, sir. Have your lawyers prepare the paperwork and send them to mine as soon as possible. Good night, sir." With that,

Kai hung up.

"Did you just adopt me?" Cassiana asked, sounding a little shell-shocked.

"Technically I just gained custody of you till you're eighteen. I'm still your sister."

"So I don't get to call you Mama Kai or anything?" Cassiana asked as they opened the back of the Navigator.

"Not if you want to keep breathing," Kai said, giving her a narrowed look.

Cassiana laughed. "Okay, okay, we'll stick with KaiMarou," she said as they headed inside.

"Can we negotiate on that?" Kai asked, setting bags on the counter in the kitchen.

"Nope."

Kai shook her head. And before she could head back to the car for more groceries she was hit with the full-on assault of a teenager hugging her tightly.

"Thank you, Kai," Cassiana said, her voice small from the tears clogging her throat.

Kai wrapped her arms around the girl, kissing her on the top of the head and hugging her tight. "What else was I going to do?" she said softly.

"You could have done anything but what you did."

"Not anything else and have lived with myself after, no," Kai said, shaking her head. "You're meant to be here—you were meant to find me, Cass. I know that. Fate has her ways."

"Well, I'm glad she decided to put me with you," Cassiana said, hugging Kai again. "Because I love you, sis."

Kai smiled down at the much lighter version of herself. "I love you too, Cass."

Kai was ready to chew nails. Fuck with me, fine, *she thought,* but fuck with dogs and my people? I don't think so!

It was the only thing that would send her to the colonel's office voluntarily. She was called into Kathy Binder's office far too often and she was sick of it. The woman was relentless—she wanted her for a lover and Kai had very politely declined. The last thing she wanted to get into the middle of was some straight-marriage sex game. They could find someone else for that. Ever since then she'd been on report she didn't know how many times, for bullshit the woman made up in her head. She'd refused to sign any and all reports, not even willing to acknowledge that they existed.

She rapped sharply on the colonel's door, waiting for a response that took far too long to come. When she was given permission to enter she stepped through the door and stood at attention with a sharp salute, the tip of her right forefinger barely touching her eyebrow. Unfortunately, she had to hold the salute until the colonel felt it necessary to return it, which, since she could easily sense Kai's ire, took a while. Kai gritted her teeth in an effort to keep her arm from shaking. The last thing she wanted was for Kathy to see her weak.

After twenty minutes the colonel finally returned the salute. As Kai put her arm down she knew she'd be paying for that in pain later.

"What is it, Temple?" Kathy snapped.

Kai held up the sheaf of papers in her hand. "Ma'am, why were these requisitions denied?"

Kathy looked up, her eyes narrowing "What did you say, Marine?"

"Why aren't you approving my requisitions for food for my crew and dogs?" Kai asked, staring straight ahead, never making eye contact.

"Are you trying to say I'm not doing my job, Marine?" Kathy said, her voice calm, but Kai could sense the underlying threat.

"Perhaps you overlooked it, ma'am," she offered evenly.

Kathy was silent for a long moment, then flicked her hand in a dismissive gesture. "I'm thinking about going in a different direction for your program."

"Did this direction include food?" Kai asked before she could stop herself, the acid in her tone unmistakable.

Like a flash Kathy was up in her face—not an easy feat since Kathy was shorter by a good three inches. Regardless, Kai got a good dose of ice-blue eyes staring directly into hers. Kathy was standing extremely close, so close that Kai could feel her body heat through the thin material of her tank top.

"You got something to say, Temple?" Kathy growled.

Kai had finally had it. Her dark eyes dropped to Kathy's, an angry fire in them.

"Yeah, I do, as a matter of fact," she said, shifting forward slightly, using her height and stronger build to her advantage. "If you want to get laid, that's one thing, but if you think you're going to use my men and my dogs to do it, you're wrong. Your behavior is beyond reprehensible at this point, and using the fact that my reporting you would only out me too is worse. You need to get your shit together, lady, because right now you're no better than them." Kai said the last stabbing her finger toward the outer offices where many men worked.

Her lips twitched apart, exposing perfectly white, even teeth and also the fact that they were clenched in fury. She tilted back on her heels and steeled herself for what would come next. She was actually surprised when Kathy began to laugh. Her dark eyes widened as she thought that maybe the Middle Eastern sun had finally gotten to the woman.

"Well, it's about time!" Kathy said wryly. "I knew you had a pair in those BDUs, I just hadn't seen them yet."

Kai raised an eyebrow. "Ma'am?"

"I've confused you? With your IQ, I didn't think that was possible."

"I assure you, I can still be baffled quite adequately," Kai said, narrowing her eyes.

Kathy shook her head. "Even in confusion you talk smarter than half the generals around here."

"Ma'am, are you going to sign the requisitions or not?" Kai asked with a sigh, too tired to play word games with the woman. She hoped she hadn't just put a major dent in her career with her outburst.

Once again Kathy stunned her by moving close, pressing her body against Kai's. Kai was further stunned to feel her body reacting instantly.

"I think we're both going to get what we want," Kathy said, noticing Kai's tension—and the hard nipples through her tank top.

Reaching past Kai, Kathy locked her office door. With her other hand she stroked a thumb over a hard nipple and heard Kai's instant intake of breath—that was when she knew she had her. Twenty minutes later she found that rather than having Kai bend her over her desk, she much preferred mounting the strong lieutenant colonel on her couch—but there was time for everything.

Such was the beginning of their relationship.

The following weekend, Kai was having what she considered an off day. She'd hit the gym in the morning, and had found that she just couldn't get into a good groove. After what would have killed normal people—but barely left Kai winded—she gave up and grabbed her towel. She signaled Cassiana and headed out to the Navigator. Cassiana joined her a few minutes later.

"That wasn't the two hours you talked about," Cassiana said, giving Kai a searching look.

Kai shook her head. "Yeah, I wasn't feelin' it today."

"That actually happens with you?" Cassiana asked, grinning at her sister.

"Just get in the truck, smart ass," Kai said, giving her a dirty look.

Half an hour later, Kai was in the shower at the house.

"Kai?" Cassiana queried from her doorway.

"Yeah?" Kai called back.

"I'm gonna go over to Xandy and Quinn's to hang out with them."

"You're going over to Xandy and Quinn's house to hang out with Erin," Kai replied with a grin.

Erin was the younger cousin of Xandy Blue, and also gay and older than Cassiana by a year. Cassiana was quite interested; it hadn't become clear yet if Erin was as well. Everyone was waiting to see, and it was becoming something of a sport.

"Love you! I'll call you later," Cassiana said, laughing all the while.

"Have fun, but not too much!"

Kai heard Cassiana say something, but couldn't make it out and went back to her shower. She soaked for extra long, trying to shake off the feeling of lethargy that was continually trying to push in on her.

"Great. Last damned thing I need is to get the friggin flu right now…" she muttered.

When she got out of the shower she dried off and put her hair up in a towel. She pulled out a leather-bound zippered portfolio holder from under a bathroom cabinet. Unzipping it, she laid both sides open. She scanned the small brown bottles with colorful labels—rosemary, thyme, lavender, sage, lemon, myrtle, all high-grade essential oils. She generally avoided all things chemical if possible, something she felt she'd gained from her American Indian ancestry—she preferred holistic medicine to traditional Western medicine. Selecting rosemary, thyme, eucalyptus, and thieves, she carried the bottles into her bedroom. After putting water into a humidifier, she added drops of each of the oils; each had their own properties that would help her fight off this looming possible bug.

She kicked her door closed to keep the oil-charged mist in the room and went back into the bathroom to dry her hair. Her hair, a gift and a curse from both sides of her ancestry, hung long, straight, and jet black halfway to her waist. She knew she should just cut it and get it over with—it was consistently in a ponytail anyway—but some level of feminine vanity prevented it, so she never made it past getting it trimmed every so often. Remington had often suggested that she get cornrows like hers. "Not my style," was Kai's response every time. Now, after spending half an hour drying it left her exhausted, she was seriously thinking about reconsidering.

Too tired to even pull on clothes, Kai walked over to her bed and dropped onto it, stretching and noting a few extra aches and pains, then put her arms up over her head and settled more comfortably. She was asleep minutes later.

She didn't hear the door open; she didn't see Kathy standing there watching her sleep, appreciation and desire very clear on her face.

Kai Marou Temple was truly a sight to behold, hot in a way that was almost indescribable. All the sinewy muscle, washboard abs that most women would kill for and never achieve, arms and legs that were muscled enough to exhibit strength but without being comically large. Kai was definitely well proportioned. Her body was perfectly on display, lying there as she was. Her skin the color of dark, rich caramel with no visible tan lines against the white sheets was sexy as hell. Even asleep she was sexy, but awake with her dark eyes and bright white smile, the woman was killer—and God help anyone she was actually trying to charm!

Kathy knew full well that Kai could break just about any bone in her body without any effort at all, but she'd had to take advantage of her great luck. She'd come to the house to try once again to reason with Kai, to try to get her to listen to her. When there was no answer, she naturally tried the front door, and was thrilled to find it unlocked. She'd opened it cautiously, even calling Kai's name a couple of times. She had noted that the dogs were out in the backyard—she waved to them cheerily as she headed back toward Kai's bedroom.

Now she stood staring at the object of her many fantasies as of late. All she could think about was how badly she wanted to feel that skin, like chorded silk, against her own again. Without bothering to stop and think about how inappropriate it was, or even the fact that she was trespassing and maybe even technically stalking Kai Temple, she got undressed, her pulse racing. She knew her only advantages were the element of surprise and the fact that once she got Kai's motor running, there was no way she'd deny her again.

Kathy moved carefully to position her body between Kai's long legs, which were conveniently widespread in her prone position. She made sure not to touch her yet—if Kai woke too soon, the game was over before it had begun. Her body's screaming at her to touch this woman, to take her, was almost deafening in her head. Kai was the one thing she'd always wanted to fully possess and never seemed to be able to. Yes, she could fuck her and keep her that way, but as soon as Kai gained her wits and was able to put distance between them, that damned brain of hers worked overtime to push her away.

All at once, Kathy slid her body up through Kai's legs, pressing against Kai in all the right spots, especially her vaginal area. Sliding her hands up Kai's arms to hold her wrists above her head for as long as she could, Kathy fastened her lips to Kai's in a deep kiss. At first, Kathy could feel Kai's body respond, pressing upward to meet Kathy's rhythmic fucking movement. Then, predictably, Kai woke with a start and immediately growled for her to get off. Kathy had no intention of doing that.

Suddenly it was like riding a bucking bronco, and Kathy was on for the ride of her life. Matching Kai's movements, she bumped and grinded her pelvis against Kai's, feeling the wetness between them and knowing she had her. Kai managed to wrench one hand out of Kathy's grip, grasping painfully but desperately at Kathy's waist, pressing her closer—it had Kathy coming in wave after wave of ecstasy. Kai came moments later with a frustrated, almost mournful yell.

When Kai had awoken she had recognized instantly the person kissing her, pressed against her. Her body was already responding to the sheer erotic nature of the situation and to Kathy herself, who knew far too well the ways to excite her. For a minute she'd been ready to give in, but then that voice in her head told her she was a *fucking idiot!* Screamed it, actually—it was kind of annoying. She'd begun struggling again, finally managing to get her hand free, but instead of doing what she wanted, to push Kathy away, her body betrayed her and grabbed the object of her lust and pulled it closer to make them both come.

Kai was breathing heavily, as was Kathy. Kathy continued to lie over Kai, her body between Kai's legs, essentially topping her, showing sexual dominance. Kathy knew she needed to keep physical contact with Kai to keep her controlled until she could get her to listen. She slid her red-nailed hand over Kai's skin, enjoying the feel of it, especially when it shuddered as Kai's body responded to her. It was a heady feeling of power.

It was, therefore, a rather big shock when Kai's strong, long-fingered hands grasped her on either side of her waist and she literally hurled her away with an almost guttural yell, which turned into a yelp of pain as she grasped at her right side. If the bed hadn't been a California King and they'd been on one side of it opposite the direction Kai had thrown her, Kathy knew she'd have likely hit the wall or the floor. It excited the hell out of her that Kai had that kind of strength. She started to climb onto the bed—Kai's hand shot out, halting her movement.

"Get out," Kai growled.

"Kai…" Kathy began, her tone low and sultry.

"Get out!" Kai yelled, wincing as she did.

Turning on her side, Kai grabbed her phone, accessing her home security system. She realized then that the reason the dogs hadn't alerted her to Kathy's presence was that they were outside. Kai hit the button to automatically open their dog door, then gave a loud whistle. She heard the immediate response of two sets of paws headed down the hallway.

"Kai, just wait, just listen to me," Kathy said, moving onto the bed as the dogs rounded the corner, both immediately growling at her.

"Hold!" Kai commanded, her eyes shifting to Kathy as she moved up, wincing again. "Kathy, I mean it. Get out or I'll let them tear you apart."

Kathy reached out to touch the spot Kai was now guarding. "Kai, you're hurt. Let me at least—"

"Don't fucking touch me!" Kai yelled, so loud it had the dogs barking and growling at the object of their master's ire. "Just get the fuck out before I give them the command to rip a trespasser's fucking throat out."

"I can't move," Kathy said, panicked.

"Chip, Digger, sit!" Both canine butts hit the floor, but their tension didn't abate. "Kathy, get off my bed, and get your clothes and get out," Kai said through gritted teeth.

Kathy got off the bed and started pulling on her clothes. Kai was now sitting with her knees up to her chest, watching Kathy's every moment. Kathy was sure she saw desire and started to step toward her again—Kai's chin came up immediately, her expression wary.

"Chip, Digger... Nackt!" She used the German word for bare.

Both dogs stood, snarling and growling, their lips curled back to reveal deadly teeth.

"There's a very short span between this and ripping your throat out, Kathy. Wanna see how short?" Kai asked, her dark eyes blazing.

Kathy moved toward the bedroom door. "This isn't over..." she muttered.

"Yes, it is. Boys! Pas Auf!" telling them to guard Kathy and said " Front door!" she commanded, and Chip and Digger tailed Kathy all the way out.

Kai tracked the movement on the home surveillance cameras, and when Kathy was outside she used the remote system to lock the door resoundingly.

Kai banged her head on the headboard, shook it as she looked down at her own body. "Seriously? Did you not see who that was? What the fuck is wrong with you!"

Chip and Digger came back into the room, jumping up on the bed and moving to comfort their master. She smiled as she petted them and thanked them for being "good boys."

"It's getting so a girl can only rely on her dogs these days…" She narrowed her eyes at her own body again. *Damned traitor!*

Chapter 3

Two days later, Cassie was beside herself with worry. Kai had been sick, in bed most of the time. Cassie had knocked on her door at one point and heard her answer from the bathroom.

"Kai?" she queried, stepping into the bedroom.

"In the tub," Kai said. "What's up?"

Cassie saw Kai lying in the huge tub, bubbles around her, and she could smell all kinds of different oil scents.

"I'm really worried, Kai…"

"Honey, it's okay," Kai assured her. "It's just a flu, or something. I'll be fine soon."

"Are you sure?" Cassie asked, seeing that Kai looked almost gray.

"I'm sure." Kai smiled weakly. "Hey, I've been thinking," she said, eager to get the worried look off her sister's face. "You need to start doing some research to find a good prep school here."

"Prep school?" Cassie said, a hopeful light starting in her eyes.

Kai hadn't won the battle with their father about changing to preparatory school, so Cassie had continued in online studies.

Kai grinned; she knew the idea was just distracting enough for Cassie.

"Yeah, I want you to start looking into what's around here and see where you might want to go."

"Oh my God, Kai, that's so cool! Can you really do that?" Cassie asked, biting her lip nervously as she thought about the expense.

Kai smiled. "You let me worry about that."

"And you're sure you're going to be okay?"

Kai nodded. "I'm sure, yes."

Cassie nodded too, wanting to accept what her sister was saying.

Later that evening Cassie was sitting in the kitchen, the dogs avidly watching her eat ice cream. Kai came down the hallway and walked into the room, grinning at the boys at Cassie's feet. She was wearing her black yoga pants and a sapphire tank top with the Nike swish on it and the slogan "Just Do It!"

"They are allowed to have ice cream, you know?" Kai said, grinning.

"Really?"

"Yeah, they're allowed junk food, just don't over..." Kai had just taken a drink from a bottle of water and she blindly went to set it down. As Cassie watched, Kai doubled over, dropping to the floor and letting out a yell of pain so loud and sharp that both dogs skittered to the other side of the room instantly. They turned and ran back to Kai, even as Cassie jumped out of her chair and hurried to her side.

"Kai! What is it?"

Kai shook her head, breathing heavily and gasping in pain. "Side... hurts..."

To Cassie's shock and horror, she then passed out cold. Cassie frantically grabbed the phone and called 911.

Finley was just finishing up with a patient when the ambulance brought in another. They told her the woman was unconscious and had collapsed, according to her sister. As she walked into the area where she'd been taken, Finley immediately recognized the dark-haired woman lying on the hospital bed. Glancing around, she set eyes on a much smaller, lighter version of the woman on the table.

"Are you with her?" Finley asked her. The girl looked completely freaked out.

"Yes," Cassie said. "She's my sister."

"Her name is Kai, right?"

Cassie nodded, wide-eyed.

"What's your name?" Finley asked softly, seeing how scared the girl was.

"Cassie."

"Okay, Cassie, I'm going to take care of Kai here, but can you tell me what's been going on with her health?"

"She's been sick for days!" Cassie exclaimed, clenching her hands tightly as she trembled from head to toe.

"Get her stats, and get me current readings," Finley said to the nurses, then reached out to take both of Cassie's hands in hers. "Cassie, when you say days, how many?"

"Like three—it started on Sunday," Cassie said, seeming to calm with Finley's hands in hers.

"Okay, and when you say sick, what kind of stuff?"

"She said she had a headache and body aches… She said she had a fever and…" Cassie said, chewing her lip as she struggled to remember.

"Any specific pains?" Finley took in Kai's color, which was almost gray—she didn't quite seem the vibrant woman she'd seen before.

"She said her side hurt," Cassie said. "She thought she'd just overdone it at the gym, and then that stupid Kathy hurt her too…"

"Kathy?" Finley said. "Hurt her how?"

Cassie shook her head. "It seemed like the same spot, her side."

"Which side?"

"The right," Cassie said, touching her own side at a spot near the belly button, low and to the right.

Finley grimaced. "Okay, and what happened tonight to bring you in?"

"She doubled over and screamed in a way I really never want to hear again, then she passed out. I called the ambulance."

"Okay." Seeing that Kai was coming to, Finley moved over to her, taking her hand and squeezing it. "Kai?" she said, loudly enough for Kai to hear over the noise of the ER. "Kai?" Finley queried again, a little louder this time, putting her hand down next to Kai's head and leaning down to be heard as she looked for any response.

As soon as she got close to Kai's head, she could feel the heat emanating from her—she clearly had a fever. "Kai? Come on, squeeze my hand if you can hear me!"

She felt the faintest squeeze and nodded. "Okay, I want a work-up on her now—blood, urine, the works—and I need a CT down here right now!"

"Kai?" Finley called. "Come on, you heard me, open your eyes for me, okay?"

Kai's head started moving back and forth, and Finley could feel her tensing and starting to breathe heavily. Finally she opened her eyes, and Finley could read agony in them.

"Okay, that's good. Can you tell me what hurts?" she asked, wanting to confirm what Cassie had told her.

Kai's right hand lifted from the table, shaking heavily as she touched her side, exactly where Cassie had. She dropped her hand again, and Finley noticed her take a handful of bedsheets, grasping them tightly as her entire body shook with the effort to contain her pain.

"Kai, on a scale of one to ten, ten being the worst pain you've ever been in, what's your pain like right now?"

Kai was breathing heavily, blowing her breath out through her nose, as if she were doing Lamaze breathing. "Ten," she gritted out.

"Okay, have you thrown up at all while you've been sick?"

Kai nodded, her lips tense with the effort to keep from yelling in pain.

"Kai, I suspect you have appendicitis, and if I'm right we're going to need to do surgery right away. Are you going to be okay with that?" Finley was worried Kai would pass out again from the pain and suspected Cassie wasn't old enough to give consent.

Kai was still breathing heavily, and it was obvious she was putting all of her focus on trying to handle the pain.

"Kai! You with me, handsome?" Finley said, trying a little bit of a flirt to get Kai out of her head for a minute—it worked like a charm.

Kai's eyes opened again, widening slightly at the question, but she nodded as she blew her breath out slowly.

"So you're okay with surgery?" Finley said. "If needed, of course."

"Yes," Kai bit out, her eyes going to Cassie. "She's sixteen... She needs..."

"Okay, I got it," Finley said. "Can we call your parents."

Kai and Cassie both exclaimed "No!" at the same time, and Finley couldn't help but grin.

"They're... in... DC..." Kai said slowly.

"Any family local?" Finley asked.

Kai shook her head, gasping again as pain shot through her. Finley grabbed her hand immediately.

"Stay with me, Kai, just hold on. Can I call Remi?" she asked, receiving a shocked look from Kai.

After a long moment, Kai nodded. "Her number is—"

"I have it, don't worry. Where's my CT!" Finley yelled, growing more and more worried about Kai's pain; she was beginning to wonder if the appendix had burst. If it had, the clock was ticking.

She leaned down next to Kai's ear. "I will take care of her, Kai, and I'm going to take care of you. Just hold on a little bit longer, okay?" She looked over at a nurse. "Please take Cassie to the waiting room. Cassie, I'll be out there to talk to you in a minute, okay? Promise."

Cassie nodded. "KaiMarou?" she said, her eyes worriedly scanning her sister's face.

"I'll... be... okay... Cass," Kai said, forcing her voice to sound as normal as possible.

Cassie left then, and Kai pressed her eyes shut, squeezing Finley's hand.

Once the CT scan arrived it was quickly determined that Kai's appendix had indeed burst, and all kinds of dangerous bacteria were currently coursing through her blood.

"Let's go, now!" Finley yelled, pointing toward the door. She walked along with the gurney as the nurses moved it. "Kai, I'm going to go talk to Cassie. You're going for pre-operational prep—I'll be up there in just a few minutes. I'll be the one in the mask, in case you were worried," she said with a wink, and saw the faintest grin twitch at Kai's lips. "Get her up there now, and start a heavy-duty round of Cefotan in an IV right away."

After talking to a terrified Cassie and calling Remington to get her to come down to the hospital to sit with her, Finley made her way up to scrub in for surgery. She walked into the operation room and went straight over to the table, looking down at Kai.

"Hi, remember me?" she said, her smile reaching her eyes—the only part of her Kai could see at that point.

Kai nodded, feeling a little more comfortable since they'd started some low-level anesthesia that was taking some of the pain away.

"Okay, we're gonna take care of this now," Finley said. "I'll do my best to leave as small a scar as possible," she added with another wink.

"That's what they all say," Kai muttered softly.

"Aww, there she is," Finley said, laughing softly. "We'll see you in a bit, okay?"

Kai nodded.

"Okay, honey," said the anesthesiologist, smiling down at Kai. "Slow, deep breaths now…"

Minutes later, Kai was unconscious.

Five hours later an exhausted Finley emerged from the operating room. She was drinking from a bottle of water and did not look happy in the slightest. Taking a deep breath, she headed down to the waiting room to talk to Cassie, who was now flanked by Remington and Wynter.

Finley squatted down in front of the girl, her surgical cap still in her hands. It was obvious she'd been crying. Her eyes skipped over to Remington and Wynter.

"Okay, she's out of surgery," Finley said. "Her appendix had burst like we'd thought, and there was a lot of cleanup to do—that's why it took so long."

"Is she going to be okay?" Cassie asked, her lips trembling.

"I'm going to do everything I can to take care of her, Cassie. I promise you that. She spiked a fairly high fever during the surgery, so I'm probably going to keep her for a few days to make sure that resolves properly." She looked at Remington. "Is Cassie okay to stay with you?"

"Nan kou," Remington said, then winced. "Of course."

"Can I see her?" Cassie asked.

"I'm afraid not tonight," Finley said, glancing at Remington pointedly. "Let's see how tomorrow goes and maybe you can see her then. She's just sleeping at this point anyway, okay?"

Cassie nodded, looking worried.

Finley stuffed her cap in the back pocket of her scrubs, then reached out to take Cassiana's hands. "I promise you that I will personally see that she's taken care of to the very best of our abilities. I will take care of her myself as much as possible, okay?"

Wynter hugged Cassiana around the shoulders. "Finley is really good. She took great care of Memphis when she was badly hurt a few months back. If anyone can make Kai better, it's Finley, okay?"

Cassiana nodded. She looked overwhelmed, but better now that she'd had more assurances and knew that a doctor was going to take care of Kai, not just nurses—that helped too.

Wynter and Remington got up to take Cassiana home, and Remington pulled Finley aside.

"How is she really, Fin?" she asked, her tone no-nonsense.

"Technically I can't tell you anything, Remi. But I can tell you she's in bad shape. I've never seen it this bad before—it was a huge mess in there, which is why I had her on the table a lot longer than I would have preferred. She spiked a hundred and five during surgery."

Remington blew her breath out, nodding.

"Would she want us to call her family?" Finley asked gently.

"No," Remington said, shaking her head. "Definitely not yet, not until we know something definitive. She's a fighter, Doc. Don't count her out just yet."

"I hope she is, 'cause she's going to need to fight here."

Remington nodded. "Whatever you need, no matter what, not matter how much, you call me and I'll pay it, okay? She's got a lot to live for," she said, smiling over at Cassiana. "And that girl needs her desperately."

"I'll do everything I can, Remi, you know that."

"I do," Remington said. "Mèsi, Doktè," she added—*Thanks, Doc.*

Finley smiled and hugged Remington, her mind already back on her patient.

As Finley passed the nurses' station a few minutes later, heading for the recovery area, a familiar voice called out to her.

"You gonna go get some dinner after that marathon, Miss Fin?" Jackie said from her place at the counter.

Finley grinned. "Yeah, right after I check on her."

"She's resting. Something you need to do right now. You've been on for eighteen hours."

"I know," Finley said, feeling exhaustion catch up with her suddenly. "I'm just going to do a check, okay?"

Jackie shook her head as she watched Finley go through the doors toward the recovery rooms. Inside, Finley walked over to Kai's bed. She took her hand, checking her pulse and looking at her watch. Her eyes blurred for a second and she had to restart her counting three times.

"I don't know about you, handsome," she said, glancing down at Kai, "but our first date really wore me out," she added with a grin.

She sat in the comfortable chair next to Kai's bed, watching the monitors. Kai's temperature had come down to 103, but it was still of concern. A minute later she was asleep in the chair.

Jackie walked into the room twenty minutes later and saw Finley huddled in the chair. Shaking her head, she reached over to pull a blanket from the cupboard and put it over Finley. She checked Kai's monitors, and as she looked down at the woman she couldn't help but feel a stab of jealousy at even the small amount of fine physique that was on display. There'd been a lot of talk from the nursing staff about Kai Temple and how incredibly fit she was. The rumors had not been wrong—this woman was definitely a sight to behold.

Kai felt like she was swimming through quicksand as she came to. The distinct sensation of needing to throw up was prevalent, so much so she was afraid to actually move her head in case it would make it worse. A low moan escaped her lips as she became aware of the pain and heat.

It was Kai's moan that woke Finley. She got out of the chair quickly, moving to the side of the bed.

"Kai?" she said, taking her hand and checking her pulse as she watched for more movement.

"Mmm?"

"It's Doctor Taylor. Do you remember me?"

Kai nodded, her expression pained.

"Okay, you're hurting. What level are we talking, one to ten?"

"Eight, maybe nine."

Finley winced. "Okay, hold on." She reached for the nurses' call station button. "Jackie, can I get some help in 10B, please?"

"Right away, Doc Fin," Jackie replied promptly.

Finley could see that Kai was starting to breathe deeply again, to handle the pain. She shook her head; the woman didn't whine and cry, that was for sure.

"Kai, still with me?" she said, taking Kai's hand and squeezing it. She could still feel the heat of the fever. *Damnit.*

"Hey, talk to me. What's happening? Is it pain, is it nausea—both?"

Kai nodded, swallowing convulsively. "Both," she said softly.

"Okay, okay. We can take care of both, Kai. Just hold on to me for a second. I have some help coming."

Jackie walked in. "What do you need?" she asked immediately, seeing Finley's worried look.

"I need ten ccs of morphine. And a Zofran, fast," she added as she felt Kai's hand squeeze hers in rapid succession.

A minute later Jackie was handing her the pill.

"Kai, you need to put this under your tongue… Good, just let it melt, don't chew it. It'll ease the nausea. And I'm putting some morphine in right now, which will help with the pain, okay? Still with me?"

"How do you know Remi?" Kai asked, surprising her.

Finley grinned. "I helped a friend of hers out a while back—Memphis?"

"Cassie?" Kai queried.

"She's staying with Remi and Wynter tonight—you don't need to worry about her. You worry about you for a little bit, okay?" Finley looked over at the monitors and could see that Kai's heart rate had slowed in response to the lack of pain. Good. "Feeling better now?"

Kai blew her breath out slowly, closing her eyes for a long moment, as if she were checking, then nodded.

"Yes, thank you," she said, her voice still low.

"I need to do a couple of things right now while I've got your attention, okay?" Finley said, looking over at Jackie. "Jacks, can you get me a consent form?"

"Sure thing," Jackie said, and bustled off.

"Kai, I need to know if it's okay for me to one, call your family if anything happens and I need consent for things, and/or two," she added hurriedly when she saw the immediate negative reaction at the idea of her contacting Kai's family, "can I talk to Remi, or is there anyone else you trust more?"

"No, Remi is good."

"Great, I just need you to sign to that effect, okay?"

"Okay."

"Now, the other thing is this," Finley said seriously. "We had a lot of cleanup to do in there, and you spiked a really nasty fever during the surgery. I had you on my table a lot longer than I like to have anyone, so that's a factor too."

"I thought surgery was supposed to make me feel better," Kai said, leaning back into her pillow.

"Well, yeah, but I think you've already got a secondary infection, and that's what I'm going to need you to fight."

"It's serious?" Kai asked softly, her eyes already starting to close.

"It can be. So you're going to need to rest and just do your best to get in touch with that inner warrior of yours. Tell her to kick some ass, okay?"

"I don't want Cass to know about… serious," Kai said, her voice fading.

"I won't tell her anything I don't have to. I'll filter through Remi."

Kai nodded slowly, her eyes closed now. She was asleep a moment later.

It was two days before Kai's fever came down to a level that Finley was more comfortable with, but it hung at a hundred degrees. Kai noted that it was Finley more often than not who did her monitor checks. On day three she commented on it.

"Are you that short-staffed?" Kai asked as Finley checked the blood pressure needle on the cuff she had around Kai's arm.

"Hmm?" Finley asked, her mind focused on her task and worrying about the lingering fever.

"I thought nurses did this kind of stuff."

Finley grinned. "They usually do."

"So…"

"So, I promised your sister and Remi I'd take care of you personally, so here I am."

Kai's eyes narrowed slightly, her look assessing. "You do that with a lot of patients?"

"No," Finley answered honestly. "But we kind of run in the same circle, albeit a large one, so that makes you a bit special. So how do you know Remi?" Finley had been curious for a couple of months now, since seeing her at The Club.

"Well, I trained her for her last fight in New York, among other things," Kai said, grinning.

"Oh, wow, that was you? She was awesome in that fight."

"Well, that part was all her. I just made sure she was ready," Kai said humbly.

Finley smiled. "Well, it looks like you did a good job. Right, you're doing a lot better, but you need to rest a lot, okay?" she said with a pointed look. "You don't look like the kind of woman that rests much."

A lopsided grin tugged at Kai's lips. "I tend not to, that's true, but in this case I will."

"Good. Don't want you messing up my good work."

"Can't have that," Kai said smoothly, her dark eyes sparkling mischievously.

Finley's expression flickered, even as she turned her head to the side. "Why do I sense that you can be quite evil when you want to be?"

"Good instincts?" Kai widened her eyes slightly as she grinned.

"Uh-huh. Rest, you," Finley said, poking her finger into a very muscled shoulder.

"Ma'am, yes ma'am," Kai murmured mildly, even as she laid back and closed her eyes obediently.

Finley watched her for an extra few moments.

The woman was wickedly sexy in ways Finley had never thought she found attractive. She clamped down on those thoughts; right now Kai Temple was her patient and therefore completely off limits.

The following day, Cassiana was finally granted a visit with her sister. Remington, Wynter, and Finley had discussed it previously, but Finley had really wanted to wait until she felt that Kai was out of the woods. Remington, who'd seen Kai a couple of times while she'd been unconscious and so pale it was scary, had wholeheartedly agreed.

That morning Remington and Wynter lay in bed talking.

"I'm glad Finley is involving herself so much in Kai's care," Wynter said.

Remington nodded, a grin twitching at her lips.

"What?" Wynter asked, her blue eyes sparkling, recognizing her fiancée's expression.

"I think there's a little more to it than what we're seeing."

"What do you mean?" Wynter asked suspiciously.

"I think Finley's got a thing for Kai."

"But…" Wynter began. "I thought… I mean, that kid Finley had with her at The Club a week or so back, and the ones before and after that—I wouldn't think Kai was her type."

Remington looked back at Wynter for a long moment. "Would you have imagined us together originally?"

"I did, Rem," Wynter said, smiling. "Remember?"

Remington skewed her lips in consternation. "Okay, well, I can tell you, I wouldn't have pictured us together."

Wynter looked back at her. The woman didn't hold anything back; she loved that about her in many respects. Sometimes it damaged a poor girl's ego though.

Remington leaned in, taking possession of Wynter's lips, sliding her hand over her bare hip and pulling her closer, causing the fire to catch between them. They made love then, and Remington reminded Wynter how much she wanted her now. Afterward, Wynter smiled; Remington always knew just what to do to diffuse any situation.

"Okay, but what makes you think she has a thing for Kai?" Wynter asked, as if there hadn't been an interruption in their conversation.

"I just think she does."

"But that's good, right? Because it'll make her more dedicated to making sure Kai gets better."

Remington nodded thoughtfully. "It might do more than that, but we'll just have to see."

Wynter thought of Remington's words later that morning when they greeted Finley in the waiting room.

"Come on back, guys," Finley said, waving them past security.

"How is she today?" Cassiana asked doggedly.

"She's even better today. Her temperature is finally normal," Finley said, sounding very happy about it. "If she stays stable like this, she could go home in a few days, maybe two."

"She's doing that good?" Remington asked.

Finley glanced back at the retired fighter. "Yeah, she's healing really fast. I guess it's a testament to being so fit, huh?"

"Or good care," Wynter said, smiling at Finley.

Finley smiled, shaking her head. "No, I think it's all Kai's doing here."

They walked into the room. Kai was sitting up in bed, wearing her street clothes.

"Who did you con out of those?" Finley asked, her look pointed.

Kai grinned, shaking her head. "Sorry, can't rat him or her out."

"Oh, it was a her, I guarantee it," Finley said, narrowing her eyes at Kai in mock anger. "You have every one of my nurses, straight or gay, willing to do whatever you ask…" She shook her head as she trailed off, grinning.

"KaiMarou!" Cassiana exclaimed, moving around Finley and hugging Kai.

"Easy," Remington said. "She's still healing."

"Oh, sorry," Cassiana said, looking to see if she'd hurt her sister.

"You're fine," Kai said. "Just be careful."

Cassiana nodded. "Okay."

"How are you doing?" Kai asked Cassiana, even as she extended her hand to Remington, who took it, clapping her other hand over Kai's. "Hey, beautiful," she said to Wynter, who leaned down to kiss her softly on the lips.

"How ya doin', Kai?" Wynter asked, smiling down at the other woman.

"I'm okay," Kai said. "Better today, according to the doc here."

Finley nodded, smiling.

"She said you might be able to come home in a few days, maybe even a couple," Cassiana said. Her expression turned serious. "I was so scared, Kai…"

"I know, Cass, I'm sorry." Kai reached up to touch her sister's cheek, her expression apologetic. "I had no idea what was going on. I really thought it was just a flu."

"Appendicitis can very closely masquerade as the flu," Finley said. "So your sister wasn't wrong to think that, Cassie. Luckily we caught it in time and were able to clean up the damage—that's what's important."

"But the ambulance—isn't that going to be really expensive? I heard it's like twenty thousand dollars or something crazy!" Cassiana said.

"I don't think it's quite that much," Finley said. "But your sister has good insurance that covers stuff like that, and I can tell you, Cassiana, if you hadn't called an ambulance she may not have made it to the hospital. You saved her life."

Cassiana looked absolutely stunned. "I did?" she asked, her eyes trailing over to Kai for confirmation.

"If the doc says so, then I guess so," Kai said, smiling. "You did good, Cass, you really did."

Cassiana bit her lip, happy to bask in the praise.

"So have you been doing what you were supposed to, young lady?" Kai asked then.

Cassiana looked blank, then worried, and then blank again, shaking her head. "What, Kai?"

"Prep schools?"

"Oh, shoot, I forgot all about that. And I figured with your being sick and all, that would pretty much kill that idea."

"Well, you thought wrong," Kai said mildly. "Again, insurance covers all this, Cass. You need to find a school."

"What for?" Remington asked.

"For here in LA," Kai said.

"But…" Remington looked confused.

"She's staying here with me."

Remington seemed surprised. "And the general bought off on that, huh?"

"What's he gonna do with another gay daughter?" Kai asked.

Remington's lips twitched. She'd never liked Kai's father, and definitely didn't like that he'd dismiss her or Cassiana for being gay so easily. She looked over at Wynter and saw that she was just as surprised. Finally she nodded. "Well, then it sounds like a good solution."

Kai nodded, sensing that Remington was surprised by the news.

They talked for a while longer, but then it became evident that Kai was getting tired. It also became obvious to Finley that Kai had no intention of saying anything about it. Cassiana was avidly talking to her about this, that, and the other thing; she didn't notice the way Kai's eyelids were growing heavy, although she was battling admirably to stay awake for her sister. Finley was more worried about her patient at that point, so she stepped in.

"Okay, I think we need to let Kai get some rest," she said, using her official "doctor tone," as Jackie called it.

Cassiana looked disappointed, but nodded. "Okay, I'm sorry, Kai… I didn't mean to…"

"Cass, it's the stuff they've got me on," Kai said, her voice reflecting her weariness. "It's not you, okay?"

Cassiana chewed on her lower lip, but nodded. Then she leaned in, giving Kai a hug and a kiss on the cheek. "Love you."

"Love you too," Kai said, smiling fondly.

Remington put out her hand; Kai took it, and Remington moved in to bump her shoulder to Kai's.

"Thanks," Kai said.

"Akeyi ou," Remington replied—*You're welcome.*

Kai grinned, never sure if her friend knew how often she used Creole instead of English.

Wynter moved in to hug Kai, kissing her forehead. "Keep getting better, okay?"

"Ma'am, yes ma'am," Kai said.

The three left then and Finley turned back to Kai. "Wore yourself out a bit, huh?"

Kai settled herself more comfortably on the bed. "Probably, but she needed it."

"You need to think about you right now, Kai."

"I need to think of her too. You don't know how rough things have been for her."

Finley wanted to say that she hadn't just nearly died, but she knew it wasn't the right tack to take with Kai Temple. "Well, now you need to rest, understand?" she said, giving her a mockingly narrowed look.

"Ma'am, yes ma'am," Kai replied, grinning even as she closed her eyes.

"Is that a military thing?"

"Ma'am, yes ma'am. Fourteen years in the Marines, oorah," Kai said, her voice nearly a whisper.

Finley was surprised, but she could see that Kai was now asleep. She looked at the woman again, definitely seeing the Marine in her, and was surprised she hadn't seen it before. But it was evident in the way she carried herself, her posture always erect, even when she was sitting up in a hospital bed. Shaking her head, Finley did a quick check of Kai's vitals and headed back out onto her rounds.

Later that evening she checked on Kai again and saw that she hadn't awoken or even moved. She had indeed overexerted herself. Finley was happy to note, however, that she still had no signs of fever—things were looking good.

The next day, when Finley entered Kai's room, she saw that Kai was sitting up and tapping away on a cell phone.

"Who'd you talk into giving you that back?" Finley asked as she checked Kai's chart and vitals.

Kai simply grinned unrepentantly. "It's easier for me to stay in touch with Cass."

"And less tiring?" Finley asked, raising an eyebrow.

Kai grinned. "Copy that."

"So, Marines, huh?"

Kai inclined her head.

Finley nodded. "I can see it."

"Most people can once they know," Kai said, clearly not bragging.

"But not anymore?"

"I discharged about three years ago, but I'm still a reserve."

Finley nodded. "Can't give it up, huh?"

Kai smiled. "Once a Marine, always a Marine. So, how long do you think I'll be here?"

"Wow, so anxious to get away from me, huh?" Finley smiled to show she was joking.

Kai chuckled, a low, rich sound. "Not you so much as this," she said, her finger circling to indicate the hospital itself.

"Sure, sure, that's what they all say," Finley said, still smiling. "I'm hoping that if you're still doing good tomorrow, you might be able to go home then."

"Oh, now who's anxious to get rid of who?" Kai said, nodding knowingly.

Finley laughed.

Kai shook her head, and Finley caught the gesture. "What?" she asked, seeing the bemused look on Kai's face.

"I can't believe you've been part of the group and we've never met. How does that happen?"

"Well, I've actually seen you a couple of times, but you were… uh… busy both times."

Kai looked surprised. "When have you seen me?"

"Well, the first time I saw you was at The Club."

"I think I've been to The Club once in recent memory."

"Well, that must have been it."

"And the second time?" Kai asked, knowing easily how she could have missed the beautiful blonde that night at The Club, with another particularly lethal blonde crawling all over her.

"At Natalia's studio. I actually thought you saw me then too…"

Kai looked pensive, a whisper of a memory coming to her, but she just couldn't grasp it.

"Natalia had just smacked me on the ass and told me to pay attention, as she tends to do…" Finley said, grinning as she thought of the hot little Latina instructor, who was very passionate about her craft of getting people into shape.

"Yeah, and she wonders why us bois don't want to do her class," Kai said, grinning. "Then again, some of us would do it if she'd promise to smack us on the ass…"

Finley laughed. "Yeah, I imagine so."

Kai looked at her for a long moment. "I do vaguely recall something like that…" she said, trailing off as she shook her head.

"Well, I didn't look quite this glamorous." Finley fluffed out her mess of curls, held in a loose ponytail, and since she wasn't wearing makeup, Kai knew she was being sarcastic.

"Oh, no, I would have noticed you…" Kai said, trailing off as her dark eyes connected with Finley's for a long moment.

Finley felt her breath catch in her throat, but quickly remembered this was her patient and they were in the hospital.

"Well, you were busy," Finley said, her tone as normal as she could make it.

Kai caught that and nodded. "But I assure you, I'll notice you from now on," she said, her very white smile far too engaging.

Finley had to mentally shake herself to keep from doing something she'd be really sorry for later. "So," she said, her tone changing completely, and Kai recognized it.

"Uh-oh," Kai said, her look suddenly circumspect.

"What?" Finley asked, giving her a suspicious look.

Kai grinned. "I recognize that tone—I know I'm now in some kind of trouble."

"I hear you're not eating."

Kai rubbed her hands together slowly, contemplatively, then shook her head. "I can't eat that stuff you guys call healthy, unless you actually want me to get sick."

"It's hospital food—it's designed to be healthy," Finley said, giving Kai a narrowed look.

"It has margarine on it, and margarine is about one molecule away from being plastic, so thanks, but no."

Finley looked back at Kai in surprise, then canted her head. "So is that basically like instead of 'I Can't Believe it's Not Butter,' it's really 'I Can't Believe it's Not Tupperware'?"

Kai laughed. "I guess that's a safe way to put it, yeah."

Finley nodded. "Okay, well, look, I'll talk to the kitchen and get something done there for you, but you need to eat. Your chart says you're hypoglycemic—how have you been keeping your blood sugar up?"

"Cranberry juice," Kai said, grinning.

Finley reached over to pick up Kai's chart, then rolled her eyes. "Takes care of the sugar as well as being good for your kidneys, which I see you sometimes have issues with."

"Yep."

"Smart," Finley said, but then pinned her with a look. "But with a body like that, I know that you know that you need protein to help you heal."

Kai immediately looked contrite. "Well, let me out of here and I'll make sure I do that."

"The problem is I need to assure that, uh—shall we say, everything is functioning properly before I let you out," Finley said, putting it as delicately as possible.

Kai closed her eyes, grimacing. "Ah, got it. But I can't eat that stuff."

"Well, I'll go talk to the kitchen now. You will eat, right?"

Kai smiled. "Ma'am, yes ma'am."

Finley shook her head. "I'll check in on you later, troublemaker."

"Have a good day, Doc," Kai called after her.

Later that evening Kai was surprised when Finley walked into the room carrying a bag from a local Chinese restaurant. She raised an eyebrow as Finley pulled up the doctor's stool, which she set up high as she pulled out boxes of food, placing them on the tray table next to Kai's bed.

"What's this?" Kai asked mildly, even as her grin gave away her amusement.

"This is dinner. You and I are going to have dinner together."

Kai licked her lips, then bit them tentatively, not wanting to break the woman's heart when she informed her how Chinese food was likely even less healthy than the stuff the hospital was serving.

"Now, relax," Finley said, seeing Kai's expression. "This," she said, holding up a box stamped *Special*, "is grilled chicken with lemon marinade. No crazy MSG or anything fried, I promise." She smiled, looking pretty proud of herself.

Kai smiled. "You win—that would be pretty healthy," she said, even as her stomach growled at the smell of real food.

"I heard that," Finley said, grinning. "Oh, damnit."

"What?"

"They only gave me one fork—I know I told them two. I'm sure there's one in the breakroom," she said, setting the bag down to go check. Kai's hand on her arm stopped her.

"Did they give you chopsticks?"

"Well, yeah, but unless I'm gonna sharpen one and stab my food with it, I can't use those."

"Good thing I can then, huh?" Kai grinned as she held her hand out.

Finley gave her a quizzical look, then reached into the bag to pull out and hand her the chopsticks. She watched as Kai pulled them out of the paper wrapper, broke them apart at the base, and expertly rubbed them together like she'd seen so many others do.

"So you're one of those..." Finley said, trailing off as she grinned.

"One of what?" Kai asked, mystified.

"Those highly dexterous people who can use chopsticks, who always make me feel like a big clumsy ape for using a fork," Finley said, grinning widely now.

"You use a scalpel, Doc—that's much more dangerous. Besides, I'm two-thirds Asian—I think by some kind of law I have to be able to use chopsticks."

Finley canted her head as she opened her box of food and stuck her fork into it.

"Asian?" she said. She looked at Kai more closely, then shook her head. "I wouldn't have guessed that one."

Kai grinned as she opened the box of chicken and dipped the chopsticks in, pulling out a chunk and putting it in her mouth. She set the chopsticks down next to the box on the table tray as she chewed and swallowed.

"I'm half Burmese," Kai said, reaching for her chopsticks and taking out another piece of chicken, then setting the implements down again as she chewed.

"Burmese? I don't think I know that one."

"A lot of people don't," Kai said. "It's south of China, near Thailand. It's actually called Myanmar now."

Finley nodded. "Interesting. I've always thought you had kind of an exotic look, I just couldn't ever put my finger on what it was."

Kai's lips curled. "Always?"

"Well, yeah, I mean… the couple of times I've seen you." Finley looked distinctly uncomfortable all of a sudden. "So what is the other half?" she asked, hoping to distract Kai from her line of questioning.

The last thing she wanted Kai to know was that she'd thought about the trainer way more than she should have over the past couple of months. She'd even gone to The Club more often in hope of seeing her again. Or how many conversations she'd had with herself about why being interested in this dark-haired butch was stupid, because she didn't date butches for very specific reasons. And how her mind had reasoned with her that this woman hung out with the likes of

Remington and Quinn, and Finley did admire those women, even though they were butches. Also how she'd thought a number of times that someone like Remington LaRoché would likely be worth the trouble of some of the butch traits…

Kai saw the thoughts play across Finley's face, not sure what it all meant but filing it away for future examination.

"Well, my mother's the Burmese. My father is half Japanese and half American Indian."

Finley smiled. "Wow, that's not a regular combination, is it?"

"More common than you'd think, for families that are from the plains states here. When the Chinese came to build the railroad, they brought their children. Oftentimes a Chinese girl would be carried off by a band of Indians and she'd end up part of their tribe. In my case, my ancestor was carried off by a band of Lakota Indians and ended up marrying the chief's son, so…"

Finley nodded. "Wow," she said, grinning. "I feel so ordinary right now."

Kai laughed. "Trust me, Doc, you're far from ordinary."

"Aw, thanks," Finley said, rolling her eyes. "So, Cassiana," she began, and then thought better of asking what she'd been about to.

"What?" Kai asked, putting another chunk of chicken in her mouth and setting the chopsticks aside.

"Why do you do that?" Finley asked.

"What?" Kai said again, not sure what Finley was referring to.

"You put the chopsticks down after every bite—why?"

"Yeah," Kai said, grinning a bit self-effacingly. "Habit." She continued when Finley seemed to be waiting for more of an answer. "It's a trick when you're trying to lose weight—you put your utensils down every time, rather than holding them constantly. People tend to eat less."

Finley licked her lips, nodding. "You think you need to lose weight?"

Kai grinned. "No, it's just something I do now. I can overeat just like everyone else, you know."

"Nope, don't believe that one at all," Finley said, shaking her head with a smile.

Kai chuckled. "Well, trust me, Doc, it's true."

"I'll take your word for it."

"So you were going to ask me something about Cass," Kai said; her mind rarely let things go. "What was it?"

"It's none of my business."

"Doc, you bought me dinner. You can ask me personal questions."

"I just don't want to overstep."

"Ask," Kai said simply.

"Okay… Cassiana is like you, but different, and the conversation you had with Remi about Cassie staying with you…"

"Cass is my half-sister. We have different mothers. Apparently my dad had an affair about seventeen years ago in Iraq with one of his clerks, and Cass was the result."

"Oh," Finley said, nodding. "That explains why she looks like you, but not totally like you."

"Well, yeah, her mom's white."

"Did your dad know about her?" Finley asked, having gotten the distinct impression that a lot of this was new.

"No, her mom showed up on my parents' doorstep about two years ago with a court order for back child support and DNA evidence to prove she was my dad's."

"Oh my... How did that go over?"

Kai shrugged. "My mother wouldn't bat an eyelash if my father had Adolf Hitler over for dinner one night, so she didn't react, as far as I can tell."

"And your father?"

"Said he wanted Cassiana to stay with them. Cassie's mom was being assigned to Turkey, and basically my father is a cheap son of a bitch and didn't want to pay any more child support. So Cass moved in."

"Just like that?"

Kai nodded. "Except that my mother hates her, and my father basically ignores her—girls are useless to him."

Finley narrowed her eyes, having sensed a sore spot in that statement, but decided not to push her luck. "She's lucky she has you. But you said they're in DC."

"They are. Cass used my dad's credit card to get a plane ticket to come meet me."

"Meet you?" Finley asked, confused again.

"I had never met her in person. She found my email address in my mom's address book and wrote me—that's how we started talking."

"Why did she have to 'use' your dad's credit card—wouldn't he buy her a ticket?"

"Sure, probably, if he'd ever wanted her to meet me—which he didn't."

"Why not?" Finley said, then remembered what Kai had said to Remington. "Because you're gay?"

Kai inclined her head. "He's very traditional," she said with a wry grin.

"So traditional he had an affair and a love child," Finley snapped, then realized she'd just insulted Kai. "Oh, God, Kai, I'm sorry…"

Kai laughed, shaking her head. "Nothing to be sorry for, because you're right, he's a complete hypocrite."

"Is that why he's giving you custody of Cassiana? She's gay too?" Finley asked gently.

"Yeah. Poor kid, it's like no one wants her."

"But you did—do."

"Well, she's my blood. How could I ignore that?"

"Well, your father and her own mother certainly seem to be able to do it just fine."

Kai grinned. "That's because they suck as human beings."

"Well said." Finley smiled, then glanced at the time. "Crap, dinner is long over. I better get back to work."

She stood and stretched, and Kai did her best not to watch too avidly, but it was definitely difficult. The woman certainly had a body under those scrubs, and now that Kai was feeling more human, she was noticing it more and more.

"Doc," she said as Finley started packing up the containers.

Finley glanced up. "Hmm?"

"Thank you," Kai said very sincerely, looking directly into Finley's eyes. "Not just for dinner—although you really didn't need to go so far out of your way—but because I know you've been spending a lot more time with me than you should with your patients, and I appreciate it. I really do."

Finley pressed her lips together, feeling the warmth of sincere gratitude wash over her. It was rare that people truly thanked her for her work. And yes, she had been spending extra time checking on Kai, but truly it was her job.

"Hey, I had a great dinner conversation for once," she said, smiling. "You're good company."

Kai grinned. "Well, maybe we can do it again on the outside."

"I might just hold you to that," Finley said, winking.

"I'm counting on it."

Finley left the room feeling completely dazed. *My God, this woman is just smoother than baby oil on a hot summer day.* She had a way of making Finley feel smart and funny, and also left her craving just a little more—more information, another smile, another laugh, another deep chuckle… It was crazy, and Finley was fairly sure she was nuts for even considering going out with her. But she was, and there was no denying that at all.

Finley left the hospital that night thinking that it would almost be sad to see Kai released in the morning; she'd have one less bright spot in her day to look forward to. The next morning, she'd wished she hadn't thought that. Kai's condition had tanked overnight—she'd even coded out. Finley was shocked, and completely floored by the change. It was obvious as soon as she walked in to check on her. Gone was the healthy glow she'd seen reemerge; she was back to looking gray and lifeless. Finley shook her head, surprised to feel tears sting the backs of her eyelids. It had been years since she'd gotten emotional over a patient. She went over to the nurses' station, and Jackie immediately saw the emotion in Finley's eyes. She stood up and hugged her.

Finley made a point of checking on Kai constantly throughout the day. They'd taken blood and were running test after test to try to figure out what had happened. It suddenly occurred to Finley that it might have something to do with the food from the night before. Grabbing the leftovers of what Kai had eaten and running it over to the lab, she found the tech, Gabriel.

"I need you to run that blood against this," she said, handing him the box. "The blood for Kai Temple."

"Okay, I'll get to it," the young man said, and started to put his headphones back on.

"No, now," Finley said. "She's very sick, and we need to figure out why. This is your priority now."

"Okay, okay," Gabriel said, not used to her being so forceful.

Four hours later, as Finley was about to get off her shift, Gabriel came running up to her. "I've got something!"

"Let's go," Finley said, leading the way to Kai's room.

They administered the medication that Gabriel had formulated and watched it drip into Kai's IV.

"So what was it, do you think?" Finley asked, feeling a bit stricken.

"There was some seriously rare-ass strain of ginger in whatever they used to marinate the stuff—either that or it was left over from what they'd had in it before."

"Jesus…" Finley breathed.

"Her chart doesn't say anything about her being allergic to ginger, Doc Taylor. You couldn't have known even if you'd known there was ginger in it…"

Finley nodded, but didn't look convinced.

Finley spent the next six hours pacing in Kai's room, waiting for things to change. Fortunately, the fever started breaking immediately, and slowly but surely Kai's vitals improved. It was three o'clock in the morning when Kai opened her eyes. Finley strode over to Kai's bedside immediately, checking her pulse and looking her over.

"Kai? Kai, are you with me?" she said, putting her hands on either side of Kai's face and staring into her eyes.

Kai blinked slowly a couple of times, looking fairly dazed.

"Hey, handsome, are you sure?" Finley asked, biting her lip.

"Flirt," Kai muttered softly.

"There she is…" Finley said, feeling almost dizzy with relief.

"What the hell happened? I feel like I got hit by a bus again…"

"Apparently there was some rare strain of ginger in that marinade they used for your chicken—you had a reaction to it."

Kai laid her head back against the pillows. "And she's already trying to kill me…" she said softly, grinning.

Finley bit her lip. Kai glanced up and saw the devastated look on her face.

"Doc, I'm just kidding," she said, reaching out to touch Finley's hand. "I'm not even allergic to ginger—it's not your fault."

Finley nodded, knowing she needed to get over this feeling of guilt.

"Hey," Kai said, taking Finley's hand in hers and squeezing it gently.

"Okay," Finley said. "I'm okay."

"Good."

Two days later, Kai was finally released from the hospital. Remington, Wynter, and Cassiana were there to take her home. They'd even brought Kai clothes—faded jeans, combat boots, and a black tank top—and shower items so she could come home clean.

Finley walked them out to the entrance. She was very surprised when Kai turned and took her in her arms, hugging her gently, her head bent so her lips were next to Finley's ear.

"Thank you for everything, Doc," she said, her voice low. "You saved my life—I will never forget that."

Finley hugged Kai back, biting her lip to hold back the tears that suddenly wanted to come inexplicably. "I'm glad you're okay," she said, knowing that was what was appropriate; she was still standing in front of the hospital where she worked—she had to remember that.

After another long moment, Kai released her. Finley watched as they all climbed into Remington's GTO and left. Standing outside, Finley hugged herself, nodding and thinking that this had been a great outcome. So why did she feel so sad?

Chapter 4

Jackie noticed Finley's obvious drop in mood and suspected it had something to do with a certain dark-haired patient checking out of the hospital. She did her best to cheer Finley up, with only mediocre results. Regardless, she kept her eye on the young doctor over the next few days and prodded when she felt she needed to do so.

One particular prod came in the form of the file review for Kai's case. Jackie had checked it for accuracy and completeness, and ensured that all of Finley's notations on the case had been properly transcribed. When she handed it to Finley to sign off on, she commented that it might not be a bad idea to check up on Ms. Temple to ensure she was healing well.

Finley looked back at Jackie, knowing what she was trying to do. "I could call her," she said, nodding.

"Or you could go over in person to see how she's doing."

"You don't think that might be a little, um... much?"

Jackie gave her a slightly pointed look. "You know you want to see that woman again—why you frontin'?"

Finley's brandy-colored eyes narrowed. "I'm not, Jacks, it's just... I don't know that it's appropriate, for one thing."

"She's been released, Miss Fin. She's no longer your patient," Jackie said, exasperated.

"Yeah, but you don't think I'd be pushing it to use checking on her as an excuse to see her?"

"So don't use it as an excuse. Just go see that beautiful woman and tell her you want to date her," Jackie said, hands on ample hips.

Finley bit her lip. "That's the thing though, Jacks. I don't even know if that's a good idea..."

"Why not?"

"Jacks, there's a reason I don't date butch women." Finley glanced around to make sure no one was really paying attention to their conversation.

"Because you think they'll want to control you."

"That tends to be a butch trait."

"She didn't seem like that type."

Finley laughed softly. "She wouldn't have in this situation, Jacks, because she was at a complete disadvantage, being sick and all. But Jesus, she was a Marine for fourteen years—you don't think that's gonna lend itself to someone who likes to be in charge of a relationship?"

Jackie looked a little crestfallen. "Would it be so bad, having someone else be in charge for a change?"

"Yeah, it would. I can't have someone telling me what to do, not in an intimate relationship. I worked too hard for my independence from you-know-who to get into a relationship with someone who thinks they can tell me what to do. We'd just end up fighting, and I don't need that kind of complication in my life—I really don't."

Jackie looked back at her for a long moment. "You can't say you're not attracted to her. 'Cause I know you are—you were here almost round the clock some days to keep an eye on her. That wasn't just dedication as a doctor, and you know it."

Finley sighed. "I know, you're right about that. I'm really attracted to her—I'm not going to say I'm not, 'cause I'd be lying my ass off. But... I just have to think long term, you know?"

"Why? None of them pop tarts are long term. Who says you can't check things out with her and then break it off if it doesn't work? You've done it enough, I'd bet you have a script for breaking up with these girls."

Finley laughed, looking chagrined at the same time. "Not exactly a script, but a definite routine..." She trailed off as she bit her lip.

It was so tempting to go and see Kai, ostensibly to ensure she was healing alright—Lord knew the woman had probably gone right back to exercising despite her warning not to. And if she'd pulled any part of the healing incision, she could get infected. Part of her knew she was just talking herself into something she really wanted to do anyway. Jackie was right—if by chance Kai was interested in dating her and if things didn't work out, she could always break it off. It wasn't like it would be the end of the world or anything.

The next evening, after getting off shift at 6 p.m., Finley used the address they had on file for Kai and took an Uber to her home. Finley didn't have a car, unlike almost everyone in LA; she lived in West Hollywood in a condo that was literally half a mile from Cedars, so she could walk or bike to work every day.

She walked up the drive to the house, a nice-looking one-story home. The front double doors were amazing, with a five-foot stained-glass inlay in a pattern that looked like a key hole on either door.

With the light from the house coming through the glass it was a beautiful myriad of colors. It was just one more layer to this woman who was starting to seriously occupy her mind. She needed to know what would or could happen with her, one way or the other.

She rang the bell, and Cassiana opened the door with a bright smile. "Hi! You come to check up on Kai?"

Finley nodded, smiling. "Figured I'd better make sure she was okay."

"Cool, she seems to be doing good, not crazy overdoing it or anything," Cassiana said. "But it's probably good that you check on her to make sure—she always tells me she's fine, but I know she doesn't want me to worry, so…"

Finley grinned. "If it makes you feel any better, patients lie to us doctors all the time."

Cassiana smiled. "Yeah, that does make me feel better. I wanted to thank you too for taking care of Kai. It was really great of you."

"Well, that is what they pay me to do. But it was my pleasure—your sister was actually one of the easiest patients I've ever had."

"Really? How come?"

"Well, she didn't complain constantly, she didn't get mean or nasty when things weren't progressing the way we'd thought. She took everything in stride and with a lot of patience and understanding. We don't get that a lot these days."

"Well, patient and understanding is definitely Kai. She's really the most awesome person I've ever met, and believe me, as a military brat, I've met a lot of people. Kai just has a way that makes you feel okay, you know? Like nothing you do is really wrong, just different."

Finley smiled. It was obvious how much Cassiana loved her sister, and to inspire that kind of love and devotion in a teenager took someone pretty special. It was yet another point in Kai's favor; they were stacking up a bit on that side.

"It sounds like you two are close, and that's really nice to see," Finley said.

Cassiana grinned. "She's gonna be my only parent now, so we better be."

Finley chuckled. "It will help."

"Well, she's in her bedroom. It's back there, last door on the left. Can you tell her that I'm headed over to Xandy and Quinn's? And that I promise to lock the front door this time."

Finley was surprised by the open invitation into the house and the request to pass on messages. She chalked it up to Cassiana's youth and nodded. "Sure."

"Awesome, thanks!"

Cassiana was gone a minute later, and Finley stood looking around the foyer of Kai's house. She had to resist the urge to check it out, knowing she would be invading Kai's privacy if she did anything but head back to where Cassiana had indicated. Walking down the hallway, she noted the dark hardwood floors and the wider baseboard and crown molding even in the hallway. There were pictures, photographs by Ansel Adams of the Grand Tetons in black frames, offset by the pale blue of the walls.

Finley came to the end of the hall, where double doors stood open—the master. There was music playing; it wasn't overly loud, but she could recognize Sia's "California Dreamin'." She poked her head around the corner and was sure she was going to faint. Kai lay on the bed wearing black yoga pants and a black jog bra. Her dark hair, which had been bound the entire time she'd been in the hospital, lay around her head on the pillow—there was a lot of it, and it looked long. Kai had her arms above her head, her long legs stretched out with one knee bent slightly, and she was asleep.

Oh my God, she's beautiful... Finley thought, and then suddenly there was barking and growling.

She hadn't noticed the very large dog lying on the bed to Kai's left, or the huge black pit bull on the floor just two feet from her—but they'd noticed her. She froze. Both dogs were on their feet growling, and the pit bull started barking.

"Hold!" Kai's voice boomed out. She was now sitting up and looking over at Finley. "Hi, Doc," she said, grinning.

"Hi," Finley said hesitantly, her eyes still on the pit bull, terrified.

"Chip, down!" Kai commanded.

The dog immediately sat, but he still growled, baring his teeth at Finley.

"Um..." Finley said, starting to back up.

"Don't," Kai said, moving off the bed and toward her. "Don't back up, he'll only follow you. Come here," she said, holding her hand out to Finley, her eyes on the dog. "Chip, hold..."

Finley took Kai's hand and felt her tug her closer. Kai pulled her in so she was only about six inches away.

"Know much about dogs?" Kai asked.

Finley shook her head, her eyes still wide. She'd treated enough pit bulls' bite victims over the years to have built up a very healthy fear of them, however.

Kai smiled. "Okay," she said, tugging Finley a little closer. "I can tell you that he would never attack you if you're this close to me, alright?"

"Okay," Finley said tremulously. "But can't they, like, smell fear or something?"

Kai chuckled. "They can smell everything, Doc. Doesn't mean they'll eat you for it."

Finley bit her lip, not wanting to sound like a complete idiot in front of this woman, but she was completely out of her element.

"Do you trust me?" Kai asked, her lips so near Finley's ear that Finley shivered at the sheer closeness, as well as the words Kai had just uttered.

Finley nodded. "Yes."

"Okay, so listen to me," Kai said softly. "I want you to turn slightly to the side, facing me... Yeah, just like that... Now, I want you to put your right arm out, your hand palm down toward him," she added, nodding toward the pit bull.

"Okay..." Finley said, doing as Kai had told her.

"Chip, come," Kai commanded. "Now, easy, Chip," she said softly.

The pit bull walked the couple of feet between them and sniffed Finley's hand, snuffling around it a couple of times, then put his head up under her palm, lifting it with his head.

Kai chuckled.

"What does that mean?" Finley asked.

"It means, 'My head itches, can you scratch it for me?'" Kai said, grinning.

Finley laughed, rubbing the large head.

"Go for behind the ears—they love that."

Finley did as instructed, using her nails. The pit bull let out a soft whimper and sighed, sitting down in front of Finley and staring up at her adoringly.

"And now you have a friend for life," Kai said. "Doc, this is Chip."

"Chip?" Finley queried, smiling at the dog and continuing to scratch his head while he panted happily.

"He had a major chip on his shoulder when I got him out of the shelter."

Finley laughed. "Makes sense. So who's this other handsome fella?" she asked, looking at the dog who was watching the action avidly.

"That's Digger," Kai said, grinning. "Digger, come."

The dog with the beautiful light blue eyes jumped off the bed and walked over to Kai, looking at Finley with interest.

"So, hold your hand out," Kai said. "Just stand the way you are, though—you never face a dog straight on when meeting them for the first time."

"Why?" Finley asked.

"To dogs it's rude behavior. You'll never see dogs greet each other that way—it's actually confrontational to them."

"Oh." Finley nodded. "Interesting."

Digger happily accepted her pets as well.

"So, Digger?" Finley asked.

"Yeah… for the gash he dug in my arm the first time we met," Kai said, holding out her right forearm to show Finley the one-inch scar.

"Ouch," Finley said, looking back at the dog.

"Tell me about it. He bit through my flak jacket and uniform shirt."

"Uhh…" Finley uttered as she hesitated in petting Digger.

"Don't worry, it was my fault." Kai grinned down at Digger. "When we first met, I tried to touch him. He warned me off, and I just didn't get it, so he bit me. We've forgiven each other since then," she said, winking at the dog.

Finley laughed softly. "I see."

"Okay, boys, stand down," Kai said, grinning at the dogs, who seemed to know what that meant as they both moved off and went down the hall.

Kai moved away then, sitting down on her bed and pulling one knee up to her chest, the other foot on the floor.

"So, what's goin' on, Doc?" she asked, her dark eyes sparkling.

Finley looked around the room, now seeing that the walls were a mellow sea green and there were more photographs, this time of the ocean and a rocky coastline.

"Where are these from?" she asked, moving to look more closely at a beautiful shot of a wave that looked like a fan as it broke sideways in the surf.

"They're from the Mendocino Coast," Kai said. "The photographer is John Klein. He does incredible work."

"Mendocino?"

"Yeah, it's north of San Francisco," Kai said, giving her an odd look. "You've never been up our coast, Doc?"

"Mostly here in LA, unless you count college."

"Where was college?"

"Cambridge, Massachusetts," Finley said offhandedly.

"So you went to Harvard?"

Finley turned around, seeing the look on Kai's face. It wasn't the least bit surprised, but there was a definite light of appreciation. She walked over to the bed, sitting down facing Kai.

"Yes," she said. "For pre-med and medical school."

Kai nodded, definitely looking impressed. "Explains why you know your stuff," she said, grinning.

Finley smiled. "Speaking of which, how have you been feeling?"

Kai narrowed her eyes slightly, noting that Finley didn't seem to be interested in bragging about the college she'd attended. "I've been alright. Definitely tired though."

Finley nodded. "Yeah, that's the general anesthesia we used for the surgery, and since we had you on the table for so long, it's going to linger for a while."

Kai nodded, looking resolute. "I figured as much. Not really used to surgeries, so…"

"Well, that's good. Let's try to keep it that way, okay?"

"I'll do my best—I really didn't plan that last thing," Kai said with a grin.

"No one does. It's crazy that we still have an appendix at all—it's really a useless organ, basically just something sitting there waiting to create drama."

"Sounds like some women I know," Kai said, smiling engagingly.

Finley laughed. "Oh Lord, don't I know it!"

"I try to avoid those too," Kai said, her eyes sparkling.

"Probably a really good idea."

Kai nodded, looking into Finley's eyes—there was that moment when they connected again, and Finley felt her heart lurch slightly. What the hell was it about this woman, for God's sake!

"So, can I take a look at your incision to make sure things are healing well?" she asked, desperate to break the moment with some kind of distraction.

"Sure," Kai said, having noted the sudden look of panic in Finley's eyes and wondering about it, but willing to let her off without questioning her.

Kai leaned back against the pillows so she was half sitting up. Finley gave her a pointed look, since the incision was actually below the waist line of her pants.

Kai glanced down and realized what Finley was thinking. "Oh, sorry," she said, grinning as she pulled down the right side of her pants to below her pelvic bone.

As it was, Kai's incredibly sculpted abs were distracting enough, but the very definite V of her pubic bone and the muscles that also narrowed into a V were just so much more. Finley was sure she was breathing far too heavily, and her heart was pounding.

Kai lifted her right arm so Finley could see what she was doing.

"Wow, on the bed and half naked in under ten minutes," Kai said, grinning. "No one's gotten me to third base this soon in a long time." She winked at Finley with a playful look in her eyes.

Finley couldn't help but laugh. It was a rather odd situation and definitely sexually charged, considering her own thoughts. Forcing herself to concentrate, Finley checked the incision and was extremely surprised by how well it was healing.

"Jesus, you have some kind of superhuman healing powers here, Kai," she said, sounding as astounded as she felt. "Okay, does it hurt when I press here?"

Kai shook her head.

Finley touched a few more spots around the incision. Kai jumped slightly at one point.

"Okay, so there, right?" Finley said.

"Yeah, just a little sore."

"Well, that's right at the panty line, so that's going to rub a bit and take longer to heal, probably," Finley said, not too concerned. She pulled Kai's waistband back up. "All in all you look like you're healing incredibly fast."

"Well, that's good, I suppose," Kai said.

Finley hadn't moved back just yet, so when Kai sat up, she was within an inch of Finley—and Finley noticed it instantly, as did her body, which lit up with anticipation. Kai's face was just a couple of inches above hers; she saw that Kai was looking down at her, her eyes searching.

"You seem nervous, Doc," Kai said softly.

Finley gazed up at Kai, her brandy-colored eyes bright, slightly wider than normal, her skin suddenly slightly flushed.

Kai lowered her head, her lips next to Finley's ear, her dark hair brushing Finley's cheek as she said, "Do I make you nervous?"

Finley couldn't slow her breathing, because her heart was beating so quickly. She bit her lip, nodding slowly.

Kai pulled back slightly, looking into Finley's eyes, searching them. "Why?"

Finley tried to think of something to say that would be funny and wouldn't sound completely stupid, but nothing would come into her mind.

Kai lowered her head again, this time her lips hovering just above Finley's. Finley could feel her closeness and felt her breathing quicken again.

"I don't want to make you nervous…" Kai said, her lips brushing Finley's.

Finley felt Kai's hand at her waist. It was gentle, her thumb brushing back and forth against Finley's shirt, making her nerves jangle. She shivered.

"Tell me why I make you nervous," Kai said, her voice still very soft, her long, dark hair hanging around their faces like a veil.

"Because…" Finley breathed, finally able to get a word out.

"Because why?" Kai sounded like she really wanted to know, like this wasn't just a game to her.

Finley swallowed convulsively. She knew she shouldn't say what was on her mind, but was unable to stop herself.

"Because I want you so much and I don't know why," she said tremulously.

Kai's lips touched hers then, as if she'd been waiting for some kind of confirmation of Finley's desire for her. The hand at her waist tightened. When Kai's other hand came up, sliding behind her neck and pulling her closer, deepening the kiss, Finley felt her body melting and catching fire at the same time. Moaning softly against Kai's lips, she slid her hands around that incredible waist, feeling the corded muscles there ripple in response to her touch.

Lying back, Kai pulled Finley down with her, her mouth moving expertly over Finley's, sucking, yielding, and then demanding. Finley slid her hands around to touch Kai's stomach, up her chest to her shoulders, and she felt Kai's hands moving down over her ass and pulling her body closer. Kai brought one knee up as she shifted Finley's weight to her left leg so that Finley straddled her, her lower half pressing against Kai's thigh.

Kai deepened the kiss again, her hands sliding up Finley's back and under her shirt, touching bare skin. Finley found she wanted Kai's hands on her so much that she reached between them, pulling her shirt off. Kai's hand at her back immediately unclasped her bra and slipped it off, then slid up Finley's bare back, making both of them moan. Finley felt Kai's hands move down to the waist of her jeans, and she was all too happy to unbutton them and pull them off along with her underwear.

"I need to see this..." Finley said, sliding her hand over Kai's torso again, looking into Kai's eyes, heated and bright.

Kai shifted her weight again, moving Finley off her, and sat up, her back to Finley as she pulled the job bra off and tossed it aside.

Finley ran her hand up Kai's back, admiring the sinewy muscles there.

"My God, whose back actually looks like this?"

Kai turned her head to the side, looking back at Finley with a grin. "Mine, obviously," she said huskily.

Finley continued to run her hand over Kai's bare back, thinking the woman was unreal in her fitness. She'd never seen a woman with this much lean muscle, and it was so incredibly sexy she couldn't believe it.

"Did you want to see the rest, or…" Kai said, grinning.

"Oh, yes, yes, please…"

Kai stood up, sliding the yoga pants and black underwear under them off, and Finley was fairly certain she was going to have a heart attack as Kai turned to face her.

She moved to her knees, needing desperately to touch this dusky skin that looked so smooth. She slid her hands up Kai's body from her waist to her shoulders, touching and grasping at muscles as she leaned in to kiss Kai's skin at the collar bone, then her neck. She felt Kai's hands on her bare back again, touching, caressing, and pulling her closer while she still stood beside the bed.

Kai's hands moved down Finley's back again, grasping just below her ass, and lifted her, sliding Finley up her own body. Finley gasped at the extremely erotic movement and wound her legs around Kai's waist as Kai took possession of her lips again, kissing her deeply, her hands slipping along the underside of Finley's thighs, moving inward…

Finley was trembling, and she felt her entire body coil in anticipation of Kai's hands touching her. Kai did not disappoint. Her fingers found Finley's wetness easily, moving against it, her mouth leaving Finley's to slide down her neck, sucking at her skin, moving Finley against her so that Finley's extremely hard nipples brushed up and down against Kai's hard-muscled body. It was the most erotic thing Finley had ever felt, and when the tip of Kai's finger slid inside her, she came immediately, throwing her head back in the pure animal pleasure that was coursing through her body.

Still holding her, Kai moved to lay Finley on the bed and continued to kiss her. Finley pulled at Kai, wanting her weight on her, having never before in her life wanted a woman over her so much. Kai obliged by sliding her body between Finley's legs as she moved upward, her lips going again to Finley's neck, then down to her breasts. Her tongue circled tight, hard nipples, her fingers caressing her skin all the while.

Finley wrapped her legs around Kai again, wanting to pull her in closer. Kai shifted so her lower half was against Finley's, firmly pressing in all the right places as they began to move together. Moisture and heat met moisture and heat and before long they were both crying out and grasping at each other.

Afterward, Kai slid her arms around Finley and lay on her back, pulling Finley with her.

Finley reveled in the strength of Kai's body. The fact that she could so easily shift the two of them with little or no effort at all was suddenly very sexy. She did her best to not think about the fact that Kai had just topped her, and what that could mean in terms of what Kai was like in a relationship.

"Topping" for lesbians meant a show of domination—it wasn't always literal, but for Finley it was a distinct cue, and it was therefore something she never allowed a woman to do to her. However, it had seemed completely natural when Kai had done just that, and she'd been so caught up in the raw sexual chemistry between them she hadn't really thought too much about it.

As they lay together, Finley remembered something. "Um…" she said, smiling as she looked over at Kai.

"What?" Kai asked, her grin open.

"I saw something…" Finley said, reaching down to touch the back of Kai's right hip. "And I think I need to see it better."

Kai chuckled, knowing exactly what Finley was referring to. She turned over.

On the back of Kai's right hip, three inches in diameter, was a brightly colored, finely detailed Marine Corps logo.

"Wow, this took a lot of work…" Finley said, touching the tattoo reverently.

"Yeah, it took a while."

"Is that the only one?" Finley asked as Kai turned back over, pulling her back down with her.

"Yep."

Finley settled comfortably against Kai's side, lying with her head against the inside of Kai's shoulder, still amazed by how incredible the woman looked. Her jawline was strong, assumedly from her American Indian ancestors; her cheek bones were high, her skin smooth and tight. Kai's dark eyes were almond-shaped and framed with long black eyelashes, with jet black eyebrows. Her look was indeed very exotic, but in such a way it was hard to put her finger on it.

Kai was looking at Finley and thinking along the same lines—that the woman was really just too beautiful to be a doctor, with honey-blond curls that fell a couple of inches past her shoulders and her perfect sweetheart-shaped face with clear, tanned skin. Her eyes were one of her most incredible features, the color of brandy, a red-brown that combined perfectly with her blond good looks. She had something sultry about her, and Kai couldn't begin to imagine how much more beautiful she'd be with makeup. As it was, the woman was a stunner.

"So," Finley said, giving Kai a pointed look. "Why the Marines?"

Kai grinned. "Family business. Six generations of Temples."

"Wow. Wait, did Remi call your dad 'the general'?"

Kai nodded. "Yeah."

"That's pretty high up, isn't it?"

"As high as you can go, just about."

"What about you?" Finley asked, really curious about this side of Kai.

"I was only a colonel when I got out."

"Only?" Finley asked, sounding skeptical. "Isn't that pretty high up too?"

Kai shrugged. "It wasn't high enough for my father, but for a woman, yeah, it's pretty good."

Finley narrowed her eyes slightly. "Why do I feel like you're underplaying that?"

Kai's lips curled in a grin. "I don't know—why do you?"

"How many female colonels are there in the Marines?" Finley asked pointedly.

Kai pressed her lips together, her dark eyes sparkling. "'Bout nineteen."

"In the entire Corps?" Finley asked, flabbergasted.

Kai nodded.

"And you were one of them."

"Yes."

"And that wasn't good enough for your father?"

"Nope," Kai said simply.

"He thought you should go higher?"

"Yeah, except there are literally only two women of higher rank in the entire Corps, so…"

"Well, that's complete bullshit," Finley muttered.

Kai chuckled. "I agree, which is why I got out."

"But you're still a reserve?"

"Yeah."

"So wait—to be an officer didn't you have to have a college degree?"

"That's right," Kai said, nodding.

"And where did you get your degree? And what in?"

"Ah, I got my degree in General Engineering, from the US Naval Academy in Annapolis."

"You went to Annapolis?"

"I went to Annapolis," Kai confirmed with an odd grin.

"Don't you, like, have to get recommended by someone in Congress to go there?"

"And you know this why?"

"One of the many things I thought about for school when I was a kid."

"I see," Kai said, thinking the drill sergeants would have had a field day with someone like Finley, with her looks.

"So?"

"So? Oh, Congress," Kai said, waving her hand. "That was easy. My dad's a four-star general."

"Is that all?" Finley asked, her tone belying the blasé look on her face.

Kai chuckled. "It just wasn't that hard to get in for me."

"So what did you do in the Marines?"

"For about half of my time I was all kinds of things. I was a training instructor for infantry, did some engineering work with a few of the units, and commanded a few platoons. The other half of the time I worked with the dogs."

"Did you know Remi in the Marines?"

"Yeah. I never commanded her unit, but I commanded one adjacent to it, and we were friends."

"Were you two ever…"

"Oh, no—no," Kai said, grinning as she shook her head. "Not anything like that."

"Oh, I just ask because I know that Jet and Skyler were a thing in the Army at one point and all…"

Kai nodded. "Yeah, it happens, but no, I would never have endangered my commission or Remi's career like that, even if either of us had been interested, which neither of us was."

Finley nodded. "I see. Because you were an officer and she wasn't?"

"And DADT."

"Oh yeah, you guys were in during that, weren't you?"

"Most of my career was under the cloud of DADT," Kai said seriously.

"So you always had to be super careful, right?"

"Well, I usually was, yeah."

"Usually?"

"I had one major lapse in judgment, which fortunately didn't blow up in my face too badly, at least career-wise."

"Do you want to explain that one?"

"When you saw me at The Club, did you see a blonde around me?"

"Uh, yeah, the particularly nasty one with the sharp tongue?"

Kai blinked a couple of times. "How do you know that part?"

"Well, I was kind of on the patio at the same time you two were having your… uh… discussion. Unfortunately I was on the other side of the patio from you two and couldn't get inside without interrupting, so I just kind of stayed out of the way."

"So you heard everything?" Kai asked, looking a bit mortified.

Finley grimaced. "Yeah, and she was one nasty piece of work."

"Oh, you have no idea," Kai said, shaking her head. "Well, she was my commanding officer at one point."

"Oh…" Finley said when she understood the connotation.

"Yeah. So that could have cost me my career."

"But it's worse than that, isn't it?" Finley asked, sensing it from what she'd overheard that night at the bar and from the way Kai tip-toed around the subject.

Kai nodded, her look guarded.

"But you really don't want to talk about it, do you?"

"It's not a particularly proud time in my life."

"I understand," Finley said. "Seems like that's most of my love life these days," she added, looking embarrassed.

"How so?"

Finley bit her lip. She hadn't meant to say that, but knew it wasn't fair of her to clam up now, not with all Kai had told her.

"Let's just say that my dating record is lengthy but not substan-tive," she said.

Kai chuckled. "Okay, you're definitely going to have to explain that."

Finley looked pensive for a long moment, sliding her hand back and forth over Kai's stomach, still marveling at the feel of her mus-cles. When she looked back up at Kai, her expression was quizzical.

"Would you be surprised to know that you are the first butch I've ever been with?" she asked.

Kai looked back at her for a long moment, trying to decide the answer to that question. "I'm not sure *surprised* is the word for it—

curious as to why, though."

Finley hesitated again, not wanting to offend Kai with her personal issues and biases, especially against her type.

"Tell me," Kai said softly.

"Well, suffice it to say that I never want any woman to control me."

"And you assume all butches are going to want to control you?" Kai asked, her eyebrow lifting slightly.

"Don't butches tend to take charge in a relationship?"

Kai considered the question. "I think that more often than not a femme gets involved with a butch expecting them to take charge, but I don't think it's an imperative to being butch."

Finley stared back at Kai openmouthed, unable to believe the extremely intelligent, well thought out and completely logical answer she'd just received.

"Why are you looking at me that way?" Kai asked.

"Because," Finley said, shaking her head with a smile on her lips, "I'm not used to this level of conversation with someone I'm lying naked next to."

Kai's eyes widened slightly. "Should I ask what level of conversation you're used to?"

"Well, the last woman I slept with was about twenty…"

"Well, that's why," Kai said, grinning. "Can you even have a conversation with a twenty-year-old that doesn't involve the words *selfie*, *Snapchat*, *Twitter*, or *Starbucks*?"

Finley laughed, shaking her head. "I really don't think so, at least not in my experience."

"So you've been dating twenty-year-old femmes?" Kai asked, almost aghast.

Finley nodded, looking a bit abashed at that point.

"Okay, I'm about as exact opposite from that as one can get. Twice that age, and very definitely not femme. So why the aberration, Doc?"

"Wow, yeah, I have to ask you about that, are you seriously 39?" Finely remembered seeing it on Kai's chart and thinking that someone had written it down wrong.

Kai chuckled. "I am, actually. How old did you think I was?"

"I would have guessed twenty-nine, although I guess that would have made you like seventeen when you joined the Marines..." Finley said, grimacing.

"So I've got two marks against me now," Kai said, grinning. "I'm old and butch."

"You are so not old."

"How old are you?"

"Thirty-four."

Kai nodded. "Okay, maybe not too old compared to you, but certainly compared to the children you were dating before."

"Children?" Finley repeated with a grin.

"Not even drinking age?" Kai said. "Makes them children in my book."

"Jackie at work calls them 'pop tarts.'"

"Oh, Jackie, that's my girl..."

"Excuse me?" Finley said, looking surprised.

"Who do you think got me my clothes and my phone while I was in the hospital?" Kai said, grinning unrepentantly.

"That little brat!" Finley exclaimed. "She never even fessed up!"

Kai laughed. "That's between you two. But I like her phrase, 'pop tarts.'"

"Oh, that's just what I need, you and Jacks in cahoots," Finley said, shaking her head.

"So why do you feel the need to be in control?" Kai asked, searching Finley's eyes.

Finley was taken aback by the question; no one had ever asked her that. "I guess because of my childhood."

"And what happened then?" Kai asked, not one to shy away from getting to the heart of a matter.

Finley looked back at her for a long moment, unable to fathom why Kai would care and wondering if she'd sound crazy if she told her. "Let's just say that my mother was ultra-controlling—she still is. You have no idea how rough it is, having every aspect of your life planned for you and forced on you."

Kai pressed her lips together, widening her eyes slightly. "My parents are both Asian, and my father is a general. I think I might know a thing or two about having one's life planned out."

Finley was surprised by the statement, but then realized she really hadn't thought about it that way. "So how did you get through it?"

"By doing whatever the hell I wanted."

"Joining the Marines because it was the family business?" Finley asked skeptically.

"Yeah, but I did it under my own choice. I've been making my own choices since I was fourteen, which was the last time I let them make a decision for me."

"What was the decision?"

"My dad deciding to put me in military boarding school because he caught me with a girl."

"You were put in military boarding school because you were gay?"

"I was dumped in military boarding school because I was gay, yes."

"What was that like for you?" Finley couldn't even imagine such a fate.

"Painful for the first six months," Kai said, grinning.

"Because of the PT stuff?"

Kai pressed her lips together, then licked them, her expression indicating how far from right Finley was. "Because they beat the crap out of me constantly."

"They actually struck you?" Finley asked, looking stunned.

Kai chuckled. "Yeah."

"Isn't that illegal? I mean, instructors laying hands on students and all..."

Kai grinned, biting her lower lip in an effort not to flat out laugh at Finley's naivete. "I'm sure it's illegal somehow. Unless the father that put you in there is a two-star general and tells them to beat the gay out of his daughter."

Finley couldn't even formulate a response to that. She put her hand to Kai's cheek, wanting to do something to show her empathy. "I'm so sorry that happened to you," she said softly.

"It's past," Kai said, shaking her head. "I'm over it. But I don't let people tell me what I can and can't do anymore."

Finley nodded, understanding what Kai was saying. "You have to meet my mother to understand. Anyway, I guess it just made me unwilling to be controlled by anyone after that."

"Sometimes the chains we think we wear aren't nearly as real as we believe," Kai said gently.

Finley looked back at her. "You're saying I imagine that my mother is trying to control me now?"

"I can't say what your mother is or isn't doing. What I can say is that you are a successful, intelligent woman with a perfectly good mind of her own, so I can't see where the problem lies."

Finley shifted over, putting her face against Kai's side, her thoughts in turmoil. Kai could sense it and let things lie for a bit. They were both silent. Kai's hand at Finley's back, stroking back and forth, soothingly lulled Finley into sleep. Kai fell asleep shortly thereafter.

In the middle of the night, Kai heard the dogs alert on someone coming into the house. She listened, and there were no other noises from the dogs, so she knew that meant Cassiana had come home. A moment later, Cassiana stuck her head in Kai's still open bedroom door and saw the very blond doctor sleeping next to Kai. Fortunately, both Kai and Finley were fully covered at that point. Cassiana's eyes widened, but then she smiled happily, and Kai motioned for her to be quiet. They exchanged a look, and it was easy to see that Cassiana fully approved of the idea of her sister with the beautiful doctor. Kai finally shook her head, grinning, and nodded toward the door. Cassiana closed it behind her.

Chapter 5

Early the next morning, Finley woke feeling Kai's warmth next to her on the bed. She was lying on her side, exactly as she'd fallen asleep. Kai's left arm was still wrapped around her shoulders, her hand on Finley's back, holding her to her side. Kai was still asleep. It gave Finley some time to simply stare at this amazing-looking woman. Looking at her, however, led to desire to touch her. Finley found that she was inexplicably drawn to touching Kai. The feeling of silken skin over corded muscles was irresistible, and Finley was not someone who resisted urges she felt when there was no logical reason to do so.

Sliding her hand over Kai's stomach, Finley leaned in to press her lips to the hollow of Kai's shoulder. The scent of Kai's skin was kind of woodsy with a hint of something fresh that Finley couldn't identify. What she did know was that the woman smelled damned good in a very sexy, non-girly way. For some reason the fact that Kai was very butch was a major draw for Finley, like knowing that something that could be so bad for her was so good at the same time. She also found that she wanted to make Kai react to her sexually. It was a power play, and in her head she knew that, but it was something she'd already begun to crave. Kai had so thoroughly dominated their sexual interactions thus far, Finley felt like she needed to get back some of her own.

Finley continued to touch Kai's skin, sliding her fingers upward, touching her breasts but only lightly brushing her nipples. Leaning closer, she kissed Kai's skin, moving down a bit so she could press her lips to those amazing ab muscles. Before long she felt the need to lie more directly over Kai, so she levered herself up on her elbow to lean over her, and continued kissing her and caressing her with her other hand.

Kai woke to the sensation of lips and fingertips on her skin, and her body humming with excitement. She stirred, opening her eyes and looking down at Finley's blond curls as she bent her head to kiss the area just above Kai's left breast. Flexing her fingers, Kai pressed Finley's body closer to hers.

Finley looked up, seeing that Kai was now awake. She moved so that she lay over Kai, levering herself up on her hands. Kai's dark eyes widened slightly at the movement. In response, Finley leaned down and kissed Kai's lips deeply, her tongue slipping over them sensually. She felt Kai's long-fingered hands slide over her back, flexing when her tongue touched Kai's lips. Finley began to move her hips against Kai's pelvis, pressing her legs apart with her body.

"What are you doing?" Kai asked softly, her eyes searching Finley's.

Finley didn't answer. She just kissed Kai again, her mouth moving even more sensually over Kai's, her lips demanding.

"Are you trying to top me?" Kai asked, sounding more amused than annoyed.

"Are you letting me?"

"I think if I have to let you, then you're really not," Kai said, her voice low but definitely showing the effects of Finley's efforts.

"Then I guess I need to make sure I do it right," Finley said, sliding her body over Kai's, slowly and very deliberately, allowing her breasts to brush Kai's body.

Kai gave a low moan in the back of her throat, pulling at Finley, pressing her closer. Finley moaned at the feeling of Kai's hands and the knowledge that she was indeed exciting Kai. However, Kai's hands, being so damned sensual as they moved over her skin, were making Finley want them on her more, and she knew that would only serve to get her off again. She wanted to get Kai off. Lowering her body to Kai's slowly, she reached down with one hand to take Kai's arm and move it above Kai's head. Kai grinned at the gesture as she repeated it with her other arm.

"Now what are you doing?" Kai asked huskily.

"I want this to be about you," Finley said, lowering her body down over Kai's, the friction of their skin still exciting her. "So leave your hands there," she added, giving Kai a pointed look.

"Mmm…" Kai moaned at the sensations Finley was causing in her body, but also at the command she'd just received—that excited her more.

Finley lowered her head, taking a hard nipple in her mouth and sucking at it. She felt Kai jump in response, her breath coming out in a ragged gasp. She put her fingers to Kai's other nipple, circling it until Kai was actually straining against her in an effort to get her to touch it. As her fingers brushed over the hard nub, Kai groaned. Lowering her head again, Finley began to suck at the nipple. Before long Kai was breathing heavily and moaning her name over and over. Finley found that her body was responding to Kai's cries as if the woman were actually touching her.

She started to move down Kai's body and felt her tense in response. Glancing up, she could see that Kai was looking down at her, her dark eyes burning with desire. Finley grinned, reveling in the power. She shifted that last foot, her mouth hovering over Kai, her hands sliding back up Kai's body to reclaim hard nipples. She looked up at Kai again, could see that she was beyond excited. Lowering her head, she moved her mouth over Kai, not pressing too close, just enough that Kai could feel it.

"God…" Kai moaned, pressing her head back against the pillows, which she was now grasping tightly. "Please…" she said softly when Finley just continued her light exploration.

When she used her tongue lightly on Kai, Finley felt an immediate reaction as Kai pressed her hips upward, trying to grind against her. She slid her tongue over Kai slowly and thoroughly and Kai shuddered, but then Finley stopped again, looking up at her.

"Jesus, Fin…" Kai pleaded. "Please…"

"What do you want, Kai?" Finley asked, staring up into Kai's eyes as she hovered over her.

Kai's eyes connected with hers, and there was something completely animalistic in them.

"I want you to fuck me," Kai said, her voice ragged.

Finley had to control her body's response to such a blatantly erotic request. She slid her body up Kai's, her skin in full contact, pushing Kai's legs wider apart as she moved between them, pressing her pelvis against Kai's in the simulation of the act. Within moments Kai was groaning and gasping loudly in her release and that sent Finley's body over the edge as she came with her.

As they lay together afterward, Finley's body still covering Kai's, they both breathed heavily. Kai's hands came down to hold Finley against her, not wanting to lose contact, as her body still shuddered and quivered from the powerful orgasm.

"That was…" Kai said, her voice trailing off as she shook her head. "Incredible."

Finley kissed Kai's shoulder, where her head had been resting as she tried to recover from her own orgasm. She looked down at Kai and smiled. "Yes, it was."

Kai saw the satisfied look in Finley's eyes and knew it was because Finley had topped her and actually driven her absolutely crazy in doing so. Kai was more than willing to let her have that victory—it had definitely been mind-blowing. She shook her head as she thought about it again.

"What?" Finley asked.

"Only one other woman's ever been able to pull that off."

"Really?" Finley said, grinning. "Just one, huh?"

Kai nodded.

"Good to know." Finley looked extremely proud of herself.

"Don't get too cocky," Kai said, grinning. "I can't stand that she can do that to me, and I haven't truly topped you yet, so…" She let her voice trail off as her eyes sparkled.

Finley licked her lips, feeling a thrill go through her. "Duly noted."

"So," Kai said, shifting to settle Finley on her side again and turning over to face her. "When's your next shift?"

"I'm actually off for a couple of days."

"Oh." Kai looked surprised. "So, any big plans?"

Finley looked back at her, her grin seductive. "I'd love to spend it in bed with you…" She widened her eyes. "But I imagine you have a life."

Kai chuckled. "Well, I do have a couple of things to do today, since I really haven't left the house since I got home from the hospital. But if you want to come along that'd be okay with me too."

Finley smiled. "Only if you promise we can do this again at some point…"

"Like I'm going to be able to resist." Kai grinned, sliding her hand up Finley's body from her hip to her face, staring down into Finley's eyes.

"I'm hoping you can't," Finley said honestly.

"Not likely," Kai said, leaning in to kiss Finley, her hand still cupping her face.

Finley responded instantly, pressing closer.

"Mmm…" Kai moaned softly. "Jesus, you're like an addiction already…"

"Good, then it's not just me that feels that way," Finley said, putting her hand to Kai's waist and stroking her skin.

Kai smiled. "I definitely think we can check the box for 'sexual compatibility.'"

"For sure," Finley said, grinning.

They got up a few minutes later and took a shower, which resulted in more lovemaking, but eventually they were able to get dressed. Finley put on the clothes she'd worn the night before.

"If I'm going to spend any more time over here, I'm going to need to go by my place," she noted.

"Not a problem," Kai said as she made them an omelet for

breakfast. "Where do you live?"

"Right down the street from Cedars."

Kai grinned. "That's convenient."

"Saves me having to own a car," Finley said, smiling at Cassiana as she walked into the kitchen.

"How'd you get here last night?" Kai asked, leaning over to kiss Cassiana on the forehead.

"Uber," Finley said. "They know me now."

Kai chuckled, shaking her head. "I can't imagine not having a car."

"KaiMarou has two," Cassiana put in as she pulled orange juice out of the refrigerator.

"You have two cars?" Finley asked, looking at Kai.

"Yeah," Kai said, tossing pieces of ham to the dogs, who sat nearby watching her avidly, hoping for table scraps. "One for me, one for the boys," she said, nodding to them.

Finley grinned. "The dogs have their own vehicle?"

"You have to see her car to understand," Cassiana said, moving to sit at the kitchen table.

"Hmmm," Finley said, nodding. "I see." Then she looked over at Cassiana. "Why do you call your sister KaiMarou?" She'd been wondering that when Kai was in the hospital, but hadn't wanted to be too nosy.

Kai and Cassiana exchanged a grin.

"'Cause she's a brat," Kai said.

"'Cause that's her name," Cassiana said.

"It's my first and middle names jammed together," Kai explained.

"Your middle name is Marou?" Finley asked, thinking it was an interesting one.

"It's our father's name," Kai said. "Normally it's an honor given only to the first male child, but since my mother was told she couldn't have any more kids, she gave me the honor. Much to our father's chagrin," she added, giving Cassiana a wry grin.

Finley nodded, already really not liking Kai and Cassiana's father very much. "So you call her KaiMarou..." she said, trying to follow the logic.

"Because when we started emailing it's how her name displayed on the email."

"I forgot a space between them," Kai said, sliding the omelet onto a plate and cutting it in half, then handing one plate and a fork to Finley.

"So now..." Finley said.

"Now I constantly sound like a Pokémon character," Kai said, smiling at her sister.

Cassiana grinned, looking wholly unrepentant.

Half an hour later, Finley understood exactly what Cassiana had meant about why the dogs had to have their own vehicle. She was stunned when she saw Kai's Mercedes—the sleek green sports car was gorgeous, and whereas at first Finley thought it didn't fit Kai, she realized it really did in a way. When Kai walked around to put her bag in the trunk, Finley watched her standing there wearing a caramel-brown leather jacket with an open Army green shirt over a black silk tank top, her black hair hanging loosely halfway to her waist—the car very definitely fit the sleek, beautiful woman standing behind it.

"Wow, this is really beautiful," Finley said, sliding her hand over the car's hood.

"Thanks," Kai said, smiling.

When they got inside Kai hooked up her iPhone and music flowed from the speakers. She immediately turned it down a bit and grimaced. "Sorry."

"It's okay," Finley said, tuning in to the music. The song was one she didn't recognize. She glanced at the display on the phone and saw that it was Rush.

"What song is this?" she asked.

"'High Water,'" Kai said, smiling as she put her sunglasses on and backed out of the garage.

Finley watched as she tapped on the steering wheel to the beat of the music. That was when she noticed the silver rings Kai was wearing. She'd seen them before at The Club and again at the studio, not able to miss the way they flashed as she talked and gestured. She hadn't been wearing them at the hospital or the night before. When Kai shifted gears to get on the freeway, Finley reached out to touch the rings. Kai glanced over at her, grinning and obligingly holding her hand out.

The ring she wore on her thumb was large, silver, and very detailed. "This isn't a regular ring," Finley said, touching it.

Kai grinned. "No, it used to be an antique spoon. Remi gave me that for helping her train for that last fight. Well, that and a fairly nice paycheck."

"I see…" Finley said. "Should I ask how much you make?" she asked, her eyes widening slightly.

"You can. If you want to know."

"Okay, let's say I was going to hire you to train me—what would it cost?"

"For how long?"

"Let's say ten sessions."

"How long would the sessions be? Hour, two?"

"Let's say two."

Kai's lips curled. "I'm not sure you'd survive two hours with me. Let's say one," she said with a wink.

"Okay, so ten one-hour sessions…"

"Thirty-five hundred," Kai said simply.

Finley looked shocked. "Dollars?"

Kai laughed, nodding.

"You make three hundred and fifty dollars an hour?"

Kai inclined her head. "Sometimes more, depending."

"On?"

"Well, if I have to travel, like I did with Remi. Or if someone's a particularly big pain in the ass," she added with a wry smile.

Finley laughed. "Jesus, I think I'm in the wrong business."

"No," Kai said, shaking her head. "You are in the exact right business. You are incredible at what you do."

Finley smiled softly. "I'm glad you think so."

Kai narrowed her eyes slightly, surprised that Finley obviously wasn't convinced of her own abilities.

Finley glanced at the next band on Kai's index finger, an Annapolis class ring. She touched it reverently, smiling. The next one was silver with an uneven channel of red, orange, and gold running around it, very rugged-looking.

"What is this one?"

"Oh, that's an Irish designer Quinn got me into. Her name is Sheila Fleet—she does a lot of nature-related pieces." Kai grinned. "This one represents lava."

"It's really cool."

"Thanks."

Finley pointed to Kai's left hand. "Okay, and those two?"

Kai took them both off, handing them to Finley so she could look at them closely.

One was another class ring, silver, with *United States Marines* engraved on it. It had an eagle on one side and the year on the other. Finley touched the eagle. "This represents your rank, right?"

Kai nodded. "Yeah."

The other ring was also silver, with a smooth channel in the middle in shades of the rainbow.

"Is this Sheila Fleet too?" Finley asked.

"Yeah."

Finley smiled. "It's great."

"I like it," Kai said.

Finley handed the rings back as the song on the iPhone changed. Kai put the rings on even as she grimaced and rolled her eyes at the phone. Using the controls on the steering wheel, she changed the track.

"I swear to God, Memphis…" she muttered.

"What?"

Kai chuckled. "Memphis has a habit of stealing my phone and adding music to it randomly."

Finley grinned. "She does?"

"Yeah, it's her way of broadening our horizons. She does it to Remi way more often," Kai added, grinning as she shook her head ruefully. "I never know what's going to show up on here."

"Why do you think she does it?"

"I think it's her way of letting people know she cares about them."

Finley nodded. "Yeah, I think you're right about that. She actually asked me for my phone once—I had no idea why."

"Well, just know if she gets ahold of it, you'll end up with music you've never heard of before."

Finley chuckled. "I'll keep that in mind."

A few minutes later Kai pulled up to a bank, looking over at Finley. "I have an appointment here," she said. "Do you want to wait or…?"

"Can I come in with you?" Finley didn't want to intrude, but was curious.

Kai smiled. "Sure."

Kai checked in with the receptionist, who stared adoringly up at her the entire time. When Kai went to sit down next to Finley, Finley couldn't help but comment. "Did you miss the big eyes she was giving you?"

Kai's lips curled in a smile. "She's cute, but a touch too young."

"I see," Finley said, grinning.

"Besides," Kai said, reaching over to take Finley's hand, bringing it up to her lips and kissing the back of it, "I've already got someone occupying my time."

Before Finley could comment further, Kai was called up. She stood, still holding Finley's hand. Finley got up and went in with her, watching the meeting with interest.

Kai was meeting with the bank to take out a loan of $100,000 for an investment. She had all the paperwork she needed, as well as her statement from the same bank indicating that she had $100,000 of her own money to add to the investment. Finley found she was extremely impressed with how astute a businesswoman Kai was. She was no "jarhead" Marine, that was for sure. Not that Finley had thought that anyway—the woman was far too smart for that.

Back in the car, Finley glanced over at Kai. The bank had, of course, happily approved the loan. It had taken a matter of twenty minutes to get the cashier's check.

"So, can I ask what you're investing in?" Finley asked.

"The studio with Dakota, Jazmine, Natalia, and Raine," Kai said as she pulled back onto the road.

"Really? To do what?"

"Looking at putting a training gym downstairs. I'm hoping I can get Remi to come in on it with me, if nothing else for her notoriety and her MMA skills."

"Wow." Finley was impressed. "You certainly don't mess around."

Kai shook her head. "Not when it comes to money, no, I don't."

The stereo was on again, and once again a song came on that Finley didn't recognize. "Is this one of yours or one of Memphis'?"

"This is Memphis', but I actually like it."

Finley listened. The song was "Medieval Warfare" by a band called Grimes. The chorus was interesting—it actually asked, "Can you kill a man with your hands?"

"So can you?" Finley asked, looking over at Kai.

"Can I what?"

"Can you kill a man with your hands?" Finley said, still very curious about the Marine side of Kai Temple.

Kai looked back at her for a long moment, then nodded. "Yeah, I can, but I prefer guns—less messy," she added with a grin.

Finley nodded. "I see. Have you ever had to do that?"

"What? Kill a man with my hands?" Kai's expression flickered with amusement. "No, thankfully. I've gotten into some fairly nasty fights, and bloody ones too, but never had to go that far."

Finley nodded, not sure why she was so fascinated by this side of Kai, but she was, undeniably so. "How did you get into training the dogs in the military?" she asked, remembering what Kai had said about working with dogs in the Marines.

"Well, it was actually by accident," Kai said, smiling. "I'd always had a thing for animals, a 'do no harm' kind of thing. When we were on patrol through a town one time, we were confronted by a pack of dogs. Apparently the Afghanis were teaching them to attack and kill

163

American soldiers."

"Oh wow, that's nuts…"

Kai shrugged. "It's war—they don't want us there, so they do what they can to kill us. Anyway, when this pack moved on us, I couldn't let my guys kill them. It wasn't right. They were doing what they were trained to do. Fortunately, the lead dog seemed to focus on me—I guess it was like a *mano a mano* kind of thing," she said, grinning. "I knelt down and pulled out some beef jerky I had on me and started talking to the dog. I kept my guys back and told them not to fire unless I ordered it, or they'd answer to me. Not something most of them wanted to do… so…" Her eyes were sparkling. "I finally got the lead dog calm, but when I reached for him he bit me."

"Digger," Finley said.

"Yep. He's an Afghan Shepherd, and he was my first dog to train. Once I got him to accept that we weren't going to hurt them, the rest of the pack seemed to calm. We got out of there, and he followed me back to the base," she said, smiling fondly.

"So you were kind of a natural."

"I guess. But it definitely got me interested in the dogs and all that they could do. So I started working with some of the K9 units. I learned a lot, and they were eager to have the attention of a lieutenant colonel who could do their unit some good in the resource department. It worked out well, and the next thing I knew, I was in charge of five K9 units."

Finley smiled. "And you got to bring Digger home?"

"Yeah. He wasn't the property of the Marines, so he was always just my dog, but he was the best trained out of all of them," she said proudly.

"I believe that," Finley said, chuckling.

Kai's phone rang then, and she hit the hands-free. "Hello?"

"Heya, sexy," came a woman's voice. "Where've you been?"

Kai grimaced slightly and glanced at Finley, who merely smiled mildly.

"Hi, Shel, I've been sick. So what's up?" she asked, trying to shorten the conversation as much as possible.

"Well, you haven't called me so…"

Kai rolled her eyes as she shook her head. "Like I said, I've been sick."

"Well, are you better now?"

"I am," Kai said, glancing apologetically at Finley. "I, uh, have someone with me right now, so can I call you later?"

"Is she cute?" Shelly asked, predictably.

"Oh yeah," Kai said, grinning over at Finley.

"Lucky girl."

"Uh-huh," Kai murmured noncommittally. "So I'll call you, okay?"

"You better!"

"Bye," Kai said, trying to get off the phone before Shelly said anything else.

"Bye…" Shelly said, her voice trailing off seductively.

Kai hung up the phone, glancing at Finley again. "Sorry about that."

Finley smiled. "No problem. Is she cute?"

Kai opened her mouth, then closed it, shaking her head with a grin. "Sorry, it's something she asks every time."

"So is she cute?" Finley asked, amused.

Kai glanced over at her hesitantly. "Ahh, I suppose she's cute. Why?"

"Are you going to call her back?"

"Probably not…"

Kai reached over and turned off the stereo then. "I think we need to talk," she said seriously.

"Okay…" Finley said, noting the tone.

"This isn't something we established ahead of time, so I need to tell you right now that I only date one person at a time, and I definitely only sleep with one person at a time." Her expression as she looked over at Finley was very serious. "And I expect the same from whoever I'm seeing."

Finley stared back at Kai, surprised. She'd figured her for a player, simply because her looks combined with her magnetic personality would have afforded her the opportunity to pretty much get any woman she wanted. She'd assumed that was the case, which was why she'd made a point of being completely casual about the woman who'd just called Kai.

"So… you don't really… sleep around."

"No," Kai said. "I don't. I usually establish that up front with someone I'm seeing."

"Before you sleep with them?"

"Yep."

"So last night…"

"Was something I don't usually do."

"Sleeping with someone before dating them."

"Right."

"Then why?"

Kai grinned. "Because I wanted you desperately."

"Ohh…" Finley said, her tone indicating that she really liked that answer. "So you kind of threw your usual caution to the wind, huh?"

"Yeah, you kind of destroyed my caution."

"Why do I like that so much?" Finley wondered out loud.

"I don't know," Kai said, shaking her head, then reached over to touch Finley's arm. "But I need to know if you can do this or not."

"Being with you only?"

"Yeah, giving up the twenty-somethings for a while."

"Are you sure that's what you really want?" Finley asked. "I mean, if you didn't plan for this…"

"Fin, I don't sleep with anyone I don't mean to, okay? Last night happened because I wanted you far too much to wait, but that doesn't mean for a second that I had no intention of making you mine eventually."

Finley was literally stunned into silence by the admission. What scared her the most was the thrill that went through her at hearing that Kai had wanted her that much and had had every intention of seeing her and being with her.

"And here I thought I was coming on to you…" she said, grinning softly.

"I don't flirt with people I'm not interested in, Fin. Especially not when I'm sick as a friggin' dog and feel like hell."

Finley shook her head. "Boy, you hold nothing back, do you?"

Kai shrugged. "Why would I? If I want something, I go after it. It doesn't mean I'll always get what I want, but it won't be for a lack of trying, ever."

"And you want me?"

"And I very definitely want you."

Finley took a deep breath. She had no idea what to do with such honesty. She'd spent so many years playing games with women, she didn't have a clue how to handle one as honest and as forthright as Kai was being.

"You barely know me," she said, shaking her head.

Kai looked back at her, seeing the self-doubt in her eyes. "Why do you do that?"

"Do what?"

"Doubt yourself so much."

Kai pulled over to the side of the road, putting the car in park and turning to Finley, her eyes searching. "Do you know what I saw when I met you?" she said, reaching over to take Finley's hands.

Finley shook her head. "No."

"When I woke up in so much pain I wanted to scream, I saw your incredibly kind eyes looking down at me, you asking if I was 'with you' and calling me 'handsome,' and I saw that smile when I answered you. It took my breath away, and I forgot I was in pain for a minute because I just wanted you to smile at me again." As she spoke, Kai stroked her thumbs over Finley's fingers, her eyes never leaving Finley's. "Even when they were putting me under, I heard you talking to me, telling me you'd try to leave a small scar. I knew I had to say something—I wanted you to smile. When I woke up sick from the anesthesia, you were right there, telling me that I'd be okay and that you'd take care of me. That was the most amazing thing in the world to me. You were a stranger, Fin, but I felt your compassion, your caring… and I know it's not just me. I talked to Remi about you after I came home. She told me how you were with Memphis, and that you put her completely at ease even though she'd just been through hell. You have a way with people, and it's not something you should ever discount. You say you're in the wrong business—I say you're not, I say you're exactly where you need to be to do the most good with your natural talents. You are an incredible person and an even more incredible doctor—so why wouldn't I want to be around you? With you?"

Finley had tears in her eyes by the time Kai stopped talking. Kai reached up, using her thumb to brush away the tear that had escaped to slide down Finley's cheek.

"Just that, huh?" Finley finally managed through the tears clogging her throat.

Kai leaned across the console, taking Finley in her arms, holding her and kissing the side of her head.

"I didn't mean to make you cry," she whispered in Finley's ear.

Finley pressed her face against Kai's neck. "It's not your fault. I guess I just don't know what to do with so many nice things being said about me."

Kai sat back, her lips twitching. "You've been hanging around too many kids who have no idea how amazing you are."

"Maybe that's it," Finley said, smiling, but doubting it at the same time. She didn't imagine there were many women out there like Kai Marou Temple.

She touched Kai's cheek, her brandy-colored eyes lit by the sun coming through the windshield. "And I would be honored to date you and only you."

Kai smiled brightly, her eyes sparkling. "Good."

An hour later they'd dropped the check off at Dakota's office along with another written on Kai's personal account for the other half of the money. They were driving back down Sunset when Finley's phone chimed. She looked at it and let out a stream of expletives.

Kai laughed, glancing over at her. "Problem?"

"I totally forgot I was supposed to meet my mom for this stupid dress fitting today," she said, glancing at her watch. "Damnit!"

"What's the dress for?"

"A fundraiser my mom is doing. All black tie and stuff."

"What time is the fitting?"

"In fifteen friggin' minutes," Finley said, sighing. "I'm just going to text her and tell her I can't make it today."

"Why?"

"Because I want to spend my day off with you."

"I can take you to the appointment," Kai said mildly.

Finley looked indecisive. "Yeah, but my mother will be there…"

"Okay…" Kai said, her tone indicating she didn't understand the problem.

"Oh, Kai, trust me—you don't want to deal with my mother. She'd test even your patience."

Kai grinned bemusedly. "Don't want me to meet your mom, huh?"

"No, it's not that. She's just… She kind of takes up all the air in whatever room she's in."

"She's that dynamic?"

"That isn't what I'd call it," Finley said sourly.

"What would you call it?"

"Drama queen, attention whore…" Finley said lightly.

"Oh, come on…"

Finley gave her a look she didn't understand. "There's something you need to know about my mother, especially if you're going to meet her."

"Okay, give me the address of where I'm going first."

"It's Saks in Beverly Hills."

Kai nodded, grinning over Finley's assumption that she knew where that was. "And that's where?"

"Oh, sorry. Um… it's on Wilshire."

"Okay, I'll find it. So what is it you need to tell me about your mother?"

"Oh, yeah, well, she'd kind of famous…" Finley said, grimacing. "Actually, she's super famous."

"Okay…" Kai said, her lips curled in a grin.

"Riley Taylor?" She saw recognition dawn instantly on Kai's face.

"Oh, well, yeah, she's kind of famous."

Riley Taylor was on par with stars like Sandra Bullock and Meryl Streep; her fan base was immense. The idea that Riley Taylor was kind of famous was like saying the Grand Canyon was kind of big.

"Kind of," Finley said, shaking her head.

"Explains why you're so beautiful though," Kai said, smiling.

Finley bit her lip, loving that Kai had said that, but still astounded by all the other things Kai had said that morning. "Thanks," she said simply.

"Okay, so what worries you about me meeting her?"

"Well, people tend to get a little… um… starstruck around her."

Kai grinned as she turned onto Wilshire. "Babe, I work with stars all the time, and most of the time they're crying and begging me to let them quit…"

Finley's eyes widened. "In that case, please come meet my mom," she said, smiling widely.

Kai laughed. "I think it would probably be bad form for me to make her cry the first time I meet her," she pointed out. "But I can assure you I won't be starstruck."

"Okay," Finley said, looking doubtful.

Ten minutes later they walked into Saks Fifth Avenue and went up to the dress boutique. It was easy to tell where Riley Taylor was because there was a crowd around her.

"Adoring fans," Finley said in an aside to Kai, who only grinned, shaking her head.

Kai's phone rang, and she looked at the display. "Damn, gotta take this. I'll meet you over there in a minute, okay?"

"Okay."

Finley headed toward the crowd while Kai went to answer the phone, leaning on the nearest wall. The crowd had finally dispersed around Riley by the time Kai walked up. Finley was talking to her mother, but looked over at her and saw the smile on Kai's face.

"What?" she asked, noting the excited light in Kai's eyes.

Kai smiled. "I'll tell you later."

"Okay…" Finley said. "Mom, this is Kai Temple. Kai, this is my mom, Riley Taylor."

Kai extended her hand to Riley, who took it, looking extremely surprised.

"Kai, is it?" Riley asked, her lavender-blue eyes staring deeply into Kai's.

Kai nodded. "Yes."

"Is it short for something else?" Riley asked, flashing that million-dollar smile she was known for.

"Nope, it's just Kai."

Riley nodded, her tongue between her lips as she looked Kai up and down.

"Mom, could you not…" Finley said, rolling her eyes. "Kai, I'm sorry, my mother doesn't seem to have any manners at all."

"I'm sorry, Finley, honey, but I don't think you've ever dated anyone this attractive before, and she's certainly not your usual type."

"Okay, well, could you try not to run her off with your bullshit?" Finley replied sharply, even as she smiled sweetly.

Riley smiled widely at Kai. "And she says I'm a drama queen," she said, winking lasciviously.

"I tend to think you bring that out in each other," Kai said evenly, her dark eyes sparkling.

"Oh, Finley, I like her…" Riley said, widening her eyes.

"Spectacular." Finley sounded anything but enthusiastic. "Can we just do this, please?"

"Fine!" Riley said, exasperated. "You go first." She wrapped her arm around Kai's forearm. "Kai and I will wait out here."

Finley looked mutinous for a minute, but finally shook her head and walked over to the attendant who was waiting to help them.

"Why don't we sit down," Riley said, her blue eyes sparkling mischievously.

Kai gave her a level look, searching, but then gestured to the chairs in the private dressing room area. Riley led the way, her hips rolling seductively as she preceded Kai. Shaking her head, Kai wondered how often Riley came on to Finley's girlfriends, although she'd never heard that Riley Taylor was actually gay.

Once seated, Riley looked over at Kai. "So, how long have you and Finley been dating?" she asked pleasantly.

"Less than twenty-four hours," Kai said, smiling wryly.

"Oh my, very new then."

Kai nodded. "Yes."

"How'd you two meet?"

"Actually, she was my doctor in the ER about a week and a half ago."

"Oh my. My very proper doctor daughter is dating a patient?"

"Technically I'm no longer her patient," Kai said, her look bemused.

"Well, it definitely gives 'playing doctor' a whole new meaning, doesn't it?" Riley asked, her eyes sparkling humorously.

Kai chuckled. "I suppose."

Riley looked back at Kai, searching her face. "You are very exotic-looking, Kai. Has anyone ever suggested that you'd do well in film?"

"No, in my three years in Hollywood, I haven't actually ever heard that one," Kai said, her tone indicating cynicism.

"I'm not trying to pick you up. Really," she said, grinning. "But you are definitely a very hot-looking woman. If I swung that way, I'd definitely be looking you up."

"Well, I'm with your daughter, so…"

"Kai!" Finley called from the dressing room.

"Yeah?"

"Can you come here, please?"

Kai stood. "Excuse me," she said to Riley, and walked over to the dressing room door. "What's up babe?"

Finley opened the door and grabbed Kai's hand, pulling her into the dressing room and closing the door. Kai leaned against the wall, looking down at Finley. She wore a strapless bra and a long crinoline.

"Aren't you supposed to be trying on a dress?" Kai asked with a bemused grin.

"I'm sorry about my mother."

Kai shook her head. "Babe, she's fine. She's harmless."

"I can hear her coming on to you out there."

"And she's harmless, trust me."

"Stay in here with me," Finley said, putting her arms up around Kai's neck.

"Honey…" Kai said, leaning down to kiss Finley's lips softly.

Finley stepped closer, pressing against Kai, deepening the kiss. Kai moaned softly, but reached up to gently remove Finley's arms from her neck.

"Babe, not here…"

"But…"

"Babe, it's disrespectful," Kai said, her tone still gentle, but firm.

Finley bit her lip, looking upset.

Kai tipped her chin up, looking down into her eyes. "I want you right now, believe me, and this outfit isn't helping," she said, touching Finley's bare midriff. "But I don't think it's right to do that while your mother is out there. I get that you think she's trying to get to me, but it won't matter. I'm into you—just you, okay?"

Finley smiled, biting her lip. "Okay."

Kai leaned down, kissing her softly. Then she stepped back out of the dressing room, right as the attendant came up with the dress in a bag. Kai held the door for the young woman with a slight bow and a grin, then walked back over to Riley and sat down.

"Everything alright?" Riley asked.

"Yes," Kai said, not bothering to elaborate.

Riley looked over at this woman her daughter was dating. She was very different from the women she'd previously met with Finley. She carried herself with a level of confidence that was incredibly attractive. Riley hadn't strictly been coming on to Kai when she'd suggested that she'd do well in film, either—she had a great look to her that was far from common. Admittedly, it had been a great line to use on other people, but this time she'd been serious. She also found it quite interesting that Kai didn't seem the least bit awed by her and her fame—it was actually somewhat refreshing. So many of Finley's girlfriends had gushed all over her when they'd met her, and frankly it was rather embarrassing.

A few minutes later, Finley walked out of the dressing room wearing a floor-length gown. Her hair was casually piled on top of her head, her curls hanging loosely around her face. The gown was a beautiful Marchesa, form-fitting in a mermaid style. It was flesh-colored silk overlaid by incredibly detailed burgundy appliques, giving the illusion of a neckline that plunged to Finley's waist while still covering everything, but outlined the very definite rounding of perfectly shaped breasts. The back was further appliqued with burgundy detail, with a cut-out keyhole. The skirt flared at the knees with even more appliques. Kai found herself completely speechless as Finley turned to look in the mirror, then looked back at her. Kai stepped up onto the dais Finley stood on, standing behind her and looking over her head at her in the mirror.

"My God, you are so beautiful..." Kai breathed, her dark eyes staring into Finley's through the mirror.

"You like it?" Finley asked, biting her lip at the look of awe reflected on Kai's face. She'd never seen that turned on her by anyone before.

"That's the most incredible dress I've ever seen, and it looks like it was made for you."

Finley turned, putting her arms up around Kai's neck and kissing her. Kai slid her arms around Finley's waist, sensing that Finley was feeling emotional suddenly. She didn't understand it, but knew she needed to be comforted. Kai hugged Finley close, one hand at her back, the other behind her head. They stood that way for a few minutes. People passing by were struck by the sight of the two women embracing, and smiled at it. Riley Taylor smiled warmly as well, thinking that Finley had finally found herself a good one in Kai. She just hoped her stubborn, headstrong daughter was smart enough to hold on to her.

When Finley finally lifted her head to look up at Kai, she smiled. "Thank you," she said softly.

"Always."

After Riley's fitting, Riley suggested that they have lunch. They decided on the Polo Lounge, one of Beverly Hill's most iconic restaurants, with its green-and-white-striped awnings. After they were seated, Riley had to sign a couple of autographs for fans.

"So, what is this fundraiser for?" Kai asked, leaning back comfortably in her chair and resting her hand on the arm of Finley's.

"It's for the ASPCA," Riley said. "It's one of my pet projects, you could say."

Kai nodded. "It's a good cause. I'm currently working with some of the local shelters to help get more of the larger dogs out of them and into training programs for law enforcement."

"Really?" Riley said, interested instantly. "What kind of training programs?"

"Well, retraining them to be search dogs, so that they can be used by law enforcement in their endeavors."

"Can you do that, though? I mean, I thought K9s were specifically bred..." Riley said, sounding doubtful.

"Ma'am, I've retrained dogs that were trained to kill American soldiers. Any dog can be trained given the right motivation."

"Kai was a Marine, Mom," Finley put in.

Riley looked surprised. "You were?"

Kai nodded. "Yes, ma'am."

"And you trained dogs there?"

"Among other things," Kai said, grinning.

"So are you working with any law enforcement groups specifically?"

"Right now I'm working on a deal with the State Department of Justice."

Riley was finding Kai Temple more and more fascinating. "And what kind of deal is that?"

"To select, train, and provide dogs for search and seizure operations."

"And how much is that going to cost them?" Riley asked pensively.

"Mom!" Finley exclaimed. "That's none of your business."

Kai chuckled, putting her hand on Finley's leg. "It's fine. I'm charging them five thousand dollars a dog."

Riley looked back at Kai for a long moment. "How much are those specially bred K9s?"

"'Bout twenty K."

"So you're really not going to make anything on this deal…" Riley said quizzically.

"It's not about the money," Kai said simply.

Riley looked surprised, but nodded. This woman was definitely not what she'd expected. She smiled. "Well, maybe if my daughter is smart enough to hang on to you, you can be her date for the fundraiser."

"That'll be up to her," Kai said, glancing at Finley and winking.

When the waitress came up, Riley ordered champagne and an assortment of meats and cheeses. Kai ordered a salad and water. Finley noticed her mother was slightly agog at this.

"Kai's a personal trainer, Mom. She's pretty careful with what she eats."

"Oh, you're a physical trainer too," Riley said, nodding. "Now I understand why you look so fit."

Kai smiled.

"Have you ever trained anyone famous?" Riley asked.

"Depends on what kind of famous you're talking about," Kai said, taking a drink of her water.

"Like well known."

"She trained Remington LaRoché before her last fight in New York," Finley said, not wanting her mom to think that Kai was just some run-of-the-mill gym-rat "trainer."

"Really?" Riley looked impressed.

Kai nodded, glancing over at Finley. "And it looks like I'm going to be working with BJ Sparks before this new tour he's got coming up."

"That was the call, wasn't it?" Finley asked, widening her eyes.

"Yep," Kai said, grinning.

"Oh my God! That's awesome!"

"You're going to train BJ Sparks?" Riley asked. "The BJ Sparks?"

Kai's expression flickered as she fought the urge to say that as far as she knew there was only one BJ Sparks, but she just nodded.

"Okay, so you're like a major trainer, then," Riley said, Kai's status rising once again in her eyes.

Kai didn't answer, simply looked back at her. It was obvious she wasn't bothering to try and impress Riley Taylor. Riley found she really liked that about the woman. She also liked that she was holding Finley's hand very openly and without any kind of reservation. It was obvious that this woman was quite comfortable in her own skin.

Lunch proceeded with more small talk. As they finished up, Riley looked over at Kai again.

"So what got you into training, Kai?" she asked as the check came. She raised an eyebrow at Kai took the check from the waitress with a smile, then reached into her back pocket and pulled out her wallet.

"Just seemed like a good transition," Kai said as she took out her credit card and put it in the portfolio with the check.

"Transition from?"

"The Marines."

"How long were a Marine?"

"Fourteen years."

"She was one of only nineteen female colonels in the Marines, Mom," Finley said, smiling over at Kai.

"Wow," Riley said, widening her eyes. "You don't look old enough to have been in the Marines that long."

"I assure you, I am," Kai said with a grin.

"How old are you, Kai?"

"Mom!" Finley exclaimed.

Kai put her hand on Finley's to calm her, even as she answered. "I'm thirty-nine."

"Well, Finley, that's like twice the age of that last little twit I met," Riley commented acidly.

"I know," Finley said irritably.

Kai squeezed her hand gently, giving a slight shake of her head, a bemused smile on her lips.

"Have you met any of Finley's other... friends?" Riley asked condescendingly as she glanced at her daughter.

"I've met a lot of them," Kai said. "I've met special agents, cops... I've met the director for the Division of Law Enforcement for the Department of Justice, the head of the Criminal Division for the AG's office, three special agent supervisors for DOJ, two rock stars, and a few others... including Midnight Chevalier herself."

Riley's eyes widened.

"Oh, I think you probably meant the women Finley dated," Kai said, her eyes sparkling. "I thought you meant the people that she's actually friends with and who respect her a great deal for her talent."

Riley was literally stunned into silence.

"Oh my God, I've never seen anyone put my mother in her place like that before!" Finley exclaimed the minute they were in Kai's car—which was something else Riley Taylor had stared at in shock.

It had become very quickly obvious to Riley that Kai was no gold-digger, nor was she one of the silly little twits Finley had toyed with previously. This was a very serious woman who seemed to have a very definite protective nature when it came to Finley. Riley couldn't help but love Kai Temple.

"I don't think I put her in her place," Kai said, her tone reasoning. "I just made sure she understood that you're more than the women you date. The company you keep should be based on who you spend real time with, not who you slept with."

"That's how you see it, isn't it?"

"Yes. Sex is just sex, Fin. Unless there's some real feeling behind it, it's just an act, and it's something everyone needs. I don't think it's her place to judge that."

"Considering her love life, that's true."

"That bad?" Kai asked, sensing another issue for Finley.

"Always a different guy. Right about the time I'd get used to someone and think that maybe, finally... bam, he'd be gone and a new guy would show up," Finley said, looking out the window.

"Must have been hard," Kai said, reaching over to touch Finley's hand.

Finley took Kai's hand, squeezing it as she felt tears in her throat again. It was astounding how emotional she felt. Kai asking questions, empathizing and being willing to defend her was so amazing—she had no idea what to do with it. No one ever took her side against her mother—no one. Never the men in her mother's life, or the women she'd dated who'd met her mother. Even her friends growing up had always ended up on Riley's side no matter what. Kai hadn't, and it was something that left Finley feeling open and raw, but wonderful at the same time. She just didn't know what to do with all the emotions and they kept backing up on her.

Kai noted Finley's silence and wondered how hard things had really been for her.

"I think I need retail therapy," Finley said, grinning.

Kai smiled. "Okay, where to?"

"Beverly Center?"

"You got it," Kai said, taking the next turn to head in that direction.

An hour later Finley had dragged Kai into Diesel, because she absolutely loved the store and wanted to see what they had. Before long she'd picked out a jacket and boots for Kai, insisting that they were perfect for her. Kai finally acquiesced and picked them up. After looking around a little bit longer they made their way to the cashier. Kai set down the items and reached back for her wallet.

"Oh, you're not paying for this," Finley said, putting her hand on Kai's arm.

"Wanna bet?" Kai asked, grinning as she opened her wallet.

"I was going to buy it…" Finley said, reaching into her purse.

"Nope," Kai said, handing the girl her credit card with a smile.

"Kai…"

Instead of arguing with Finley, Kai leaned in and kissed her until she was somewhat breathless. Finley rocked back on her heels when their lips parted.

"Guess you told me…" she said, grinning.

Kai grinned, widening her eyes, even as she signed the receipt to hand it back to the sales girl, who was watching them with interest. Kai took the bag from the girl, thanking her and guiding Finley toward the exit.

"So where to now?" Kai asked.

"Prada. I need shoes for that dress."

They made their way to Prada, and Finley found a pair of heels that would go perfectly with the Marchesa dress. She tried them on and loved them. She told the sales clerk she'd take them, and while she was putting her shoes back on Kai walked up to the front, once again handing the clerk her credit card before Finley even knew what she was doing. When Finley got up to the counter, Kai was already taking the bag from the clerk.

"You did not…" Finley said, trailing off as she gave Kai an open-mouthed look.

Kai grinned. "I wanted to."

"Kai, those were eleven-hundred-dollar shoes…"

"I saw the receipt," Kai said, grinning still.

Finley shook her head. "No, we need to return them, and I'm paying for them."

Kai blocked her way to the counter, leaning down and kissing her lips, pulling back to look at her. "Let me do this for you, please?"

"But I didn't expect you to, I didn't…"

"I know you didn't," Kai said. "But I want to, okay?"

"Kai…"

"You're used to paying for everything, aren't you?"

Finley bit her lip, nodding. "That's what happens when you date twenty-year-olds."

"Well, it's a bad habit, and you need to stop it," Kai said, smiling to take the sting out of her words.

Finley took Kai's jacket in her hands, leaning her head against Kai's chest. Kai put her arm around her, holding her there. It astounded Kai how annoyed she was that so many of these other women had taken advantage of Finley's ability to pay for things. In her book it just wasn't right at all. After a couple of minutes, Kai reached up, taking one of Finley's hands, and led her out of the store.

Back in the car, Kai glanced over. "So where to now?" she asked with a grin.

"I think we need to go back to your house so I can thank you properly for the shoes," Finley said, smiling mischievously.

Chapter 6

Before long, Finley was spending most of her free time with Kai, not wanting to be away from her any longer than was necessary for work. Kai had gotten back into her routine of seeing clients as well as working with the dogs. They were both extremely busy, but spent as much time together as they could. Cassiana had started at Harvard-Westlake School in Studio City, with her focus on the Institute for Scholastic Sports Science & Medicine. She was seriously considering a career in the medical field. Kai thought it was directly related to Finley, and how much Cassiana admired her. Finley was very touched by the idea.

The three of them became a fairly close unit, and they all enjoyed the feeling of an actual family for a change. Things were going well.

A couple of months into the relationship, Kai was worried one day when she hadn't heard from Finley all morning. She knew she was on shift at the hospital, but something just felt off. Kai had tried calling a couple of times, and texting as well. To allay her concerns, she swung by the hospital on her way back through town from an appointment with a client.

Walking inside, Kai easily located Jackie. "Hey, beautiful," Kai said, smiling down at the nurse.

"Oh, hi there, handsome!" Jackie said, smiling brightly. She'd come to absolutely adore Kai Temple for how happy she made Finley. "What can I do ya for?"

"Any sign of my girl?"

Jackie looked surprised by the question. "Honey, she's home sick," she said. "She didn't call you?"

Kai widened her eyes, giving her an "obviously not" look.

"Well, she was pretty out of it this morning when she called in," Jackie said, glancing at the clock. "Yep, looks like it's dinnertime. Let's go, handsome—you're driving."

Kai grinned. "Where are we going?"

"To check on our girl," Jackie said, holding up a set of keys and jingling them.

Twenty minutes later, Jackie opened the door to Finley's condo. Kai had been there a few times. She looked around; the place was silent. She walked toward Finley's bedroom, Jackie following. Finley lay huddled under blankets. Kai knelt next to the bed, reaching out to touch Finley's face. It felt hot.

"Honey…" Kai said softly.

Finley's eyes opened slowly. "Kai?" she whispered, surprised to see her there.

"Yeah, babe. Why didn't you call me?"

"I texted you…" Finley said, trailing off pensively. "At least, I thought I did…"

"Nope," Kai said, grinning. "Doesn't matter—I'm here now."

"I don't want you to see me like this," Finley said, covering her face with her hands.

"Like what?"

"Sick. I look terrible!"

Kai laughed, shaking her head. "Like I looked so fantastic when I was brought into the ER, huh?"

"You did—you always do," Finley said stubbornly.

"Uh-huh, right," Kai said disbelievingly.

Jackie watched as Kai talked to Finley. Her heart swelled—this was the kind of woman she'd always wanted for her little girl. Someone who would take care of her, no matter what happened. Walking over, she leaned down to kiss Finley on the check, then kissed Kai on the forehead.

"I'm gonna head back," she said. "No, no, I can get back," she added when Kai started to stand and pulled out her keys.

"You can take my car if you want," Kai said.

"Me? Drive that Mercedes? Girl, you crazy!" Jackie smiled. "I'm good, honey. You just take care of our girl."

Kai smiled. "I will. Thanks, Jackie."

Jackie left and Kai knelt next to the bed again, reaching up to stroke Finley's forehead.

"So, tell me what we're looking at here, and what you've done to make yourself feel better."

"Cold, flu… headache, fever, chills, muscle aches, sore throat…"

"Okay," Kai said, nodding. "What have you done to make things feel better?"

Finley was silent.

"Babe?" Kai queried.

"Slept."

Kai chuckled. "Okay, well, I think we should be just a little more proactive than that. First of all, why's it so cold in here?"

"I haven't had the time to get the gas company out to check the pilot light," Finley said. The seasons were just changing at that point.

"Okay, well, let me take care of that first," Kai said, standing again. "I'll be right back."

A few minutes later the heater kicked on and Kai came back into the room. "Problem number one solved," she said, grinning. "Now, about that sore throat, do you have any tea?"

"Um…" Finley stammered, her expression blank.

"I'll go check," Kai said, and left the room again.

Finley watched her walk out and had a feeling she knew what she'd hear next. She was right.

"Seriously!" she heard Kai say. She grinned to herself, knowing that Kai had just walked into her kitchen and had started looking around for food. Kai was likely going to have heart failure at how badly she ate when she was home—frozen dinners, boxed meals, anything fast and easy.

When Kai walked back in the room, Finley was already grinning.

"You know what I'm about to say, right?" Kai said, grinning too.

"Uh-huh. But can you keep the expletives to a minimum? I'm sick, you know…"

Kai smiled at that. "Uh-huh," she said, kneeling down to look into Finley's eyes again. "I saw a market downstairs—I'm going to go do some quick shopping."

"That's a natural-foods… oh…" Finley realized who she was talking to and shut up.

"I will be right back," Kai said, softly kissing Finley's lips. "Don't run off on me, huh?"

"Where would I go?" Finley asked wistfully.

Kai was gone less than an hour. When she got back she immediately made Finley tea with lemon and peppermint essential oils, adding honey. Back in Finley's room, she knelt down, touching Finley's cheek, and set the tea on the nightstand. Finley opened her eyes, smiling softly.

"I made you some tea," Kai said. "It should help your throat and your fever."

Finley moved to sit up, and Kai stood to help her, putting pillows behind her, then handed her the cup. Finley took a sip and sighed.

"What's in this?" she asked.

"There's lemon and peppermint, and honey."

Finley held the cup with both hands, sipping at it like a child would.

"Have you had anything to eat today?" Kai asked.

Finley shook her head.

"Okay, I'm going to get you some toast to start with, but then I'm going to make you some real food."

Finley grinned. "Versus what I had in my fridge?"

"We're not even going to talk about what was in that fridge," Kai said darkly, even as she grinned.

Kai made Finley toast, keeping it soft so it wouldn't be too scratchy on her throat. She ate it, still sipping on her tea. After she was done, Kai kicked off her shoes and took off her jacket—wearing black workout pants and a white tank top with a jog bra under it, she was the picture of health. Climbing into bed, she gently pulled Finley into her arms and held her, stroking her hair, pulling the covers up to keep her warm.

"Kai, I don't want to get you sick," Finley protested weakly.

"I've done my sick for this year," Kai said, grinning. "Don't worry, babe."

Finley snuggled against Kai's chest, feeling warm and far too happy considering how lousy as she felt. She was asleep a little while later. Kai carefully got up and went back into Finley's kitchen. The kitchen itself, like the rest of the condo, was beautiful, with stainless steel appliances and every possible convenience. The food that Finley had in her house looked like it belonged in some twenty-year-old's kitchen—macaroni and cheese, SpaghettiOs, TV dinners in the freezer, old to-go containers in the fridge, soda, old wine, and a few terrifying-looking science projects Kai was almost afraid to touch. It was not the refrigerator of a doctor at all. Kai had to resist the urge to throw everything out, and not just the stuff that was past its natural life. She had to hunt around in the drawers for a knife and cutting board. The woman had almost nothing in the way of cooking utensils. Kai shook her head ruefully.

She managed to find enough things to cook the chicken soup she had bought supplies for. She added rosemary and let it simmer. Walking back into the bedroom, she checked on Finley and saw that she was sleeping still. She sat on the bed carefully so as not to disturb her. Pulling out her phone, she started moving her appointments for the next two days so she could stay with Finley. She got up a few times to check on the soup, and turned it off when she was finally happy with it.

Finley woke a couple of hours later, and Kai brought her soup and some water.

"Oh my God, this is like completely homemade, isn't it?" Finley asked as she took a mouthful.

"Versus a can?" Kai asked, grinning.

"Um, yeah…" Finley said, grinning back. "Campbell's, you know…"

Kai shuddered dramatically. "Not on my watch."

Finley chuckled. "Seriously, Kai, this is really incredible." She'd known that Kai could cook, since she'd done so most of the nights they'd been together. She knew Kai liked to use fresh ingredients and make as much from scratch as possible. They'd had a lot of discussions about why certain things that seemed healthy weren't. Finley was learning a lot.

After she finished eating, they watched some TV. Finley found that even though Kai held the remote, she brought up the guide and let Finley tell her what she wanted to watch. She only drew the line a couple of times, one of those being *Keeping Up with the Kardashians*, which Finley had only suggested to see how Kai would react.

"Uh, no," Kai said, shaking her head. "I need all the brain cells I have left, thank you." Finley chuckled.

They settled on a movie on the Independent Film Channel that Finley had picked because of the title: *A Marine Story*. It was about a female Marine who returned to her small hometown after discharging from the military. She'd discovered while in the military that she was gay, and even though she'd married a man to hide it, she'd been accused of being gay and had resigned rather than take the chance of being dishonorably discharged.

Finley had noticed that Kai nodded quite a lot during the movie. She asked a few times if it was accurate.

"Oh yeah," Kai said. "That's exactly the way it was."

Finley shook her head. "I don't know how you did it," she said, her tone pained. "How you lived like that… hiding who you really were."

"A lot of people lived that way, Fin. If you wanted a career in the military, you had to be what they wanted you to be, not who you really were."

"I'm glad Obama got rid of Don't Ask Don't Tell."

"Believe me, so are many people in the military."

"Did people know about you?" Finley asked at one point.

"Yeah, some of the guys in my unit knew, but they were cool, so it was generally safe. The problem was, there was always that chance that I'd piss one of them off and they'd rat me out."

"And when you were with her…" Finley said gently.

"Hell, I was never sure what was going to happen there. Half the time I wondered if she'd turn me in herself. She was just vindictive enough to do that."

"So why didn't you two work out?"

"You mean besides the fact that we were both in a military that forbade us from being together?" Kai said wryly. Finley nodded. "It was simple—she used me for sex. She told me she loved me, she told me she wanted to be with me, but in the end her husband had the power she needed to move up in the military and that's what she wanted."

"Ouch," Finley said, frowning.

"Yeah. The thing was, if she'd just been honest, I would have been okay. But she spun this whole tale about how he would out her if she left him, and that she needed to find another way, that she was 'working on it.' She had me so completely fooled, and I stayed that way for a long time. When I finally got fed up and broke it off, she just laughed in my face. I was so sick over it. She told me she was never really into me, that she just liked to see me twist. That she was just bored over there in the Middle of Nowhere, as she always put it, and I was a distraction."

"Not really into you? Right, sure, I believe that…"

"Well, I heard later that she moved back to the States, and divorced him and married a woman under her command." Kai had said it simply, but it was obvious it still hurt her.

Finley shook her head sadly. "I really hate that woman."

Kai grinned. "You've never even met her."

"I've never met your father, but I don't like him much either."

Kai pressed her lips together. "Tell me how you really feel, babe."

Finley did her best to look circumspect, but didn't really pull it off. She didn't like anyone that didn't see Kai as the amazing woman she was.

"How many appointments did you have to reschedule to be here with me?" Finley asked, wanting to steer the conversation away from Kai's ex. She was also aware how busy Kai usually was.

"A few."

"A lot, I'm betting. It's the middle of the week and that's when you're busiest."

"I'm where I need to be," Kai said seriously.

Finley looked back at her, her smile soft. "Taking care of me."

"Taking care of you."

Later that night Finley got the chills. Kai bundled her in the covers and went to run a hot bath. She added oils that would soothe Finley and help her cold at the same time. She turned on the heated tiles and also the towel warmers. Once everything was ready, she got Finley up and carried her into the bathroom, bundled in a thick, warm robe. She helped Finley get into the tub, then sat down on the floor next to it. She had a book out and was looking through it.

Finley lay in the tub turned on her side, the warm water right up to her chin. She watched Kai as she flipped through the book. Finley inhaled deeply, smelling the wonderful scent from the water.

"Okay, what's in this?" she asked. "Because it smells wonderful."

"Lavender, eucalyptus, rosemary, and chamomile."

"So, like aromatherapy stuff?"

"No, like actual essential oils that you absorb through your skin that will help you fight off this cold."

Finley narrowed her eyes slightly. "And this is a new side of you now too…"

"What do you mean?"

"I mean, I know you eat clean and all, but you don't take medicine either?"

"I avoid taking medicine if I don't have to. I mean, unless I've got appendicitis and I'm like dying or something," Kai said, winking at Finley with a grin. "This is how the Indians used to care for themselves—this is ancient medicine."

"So you are in touch with your American Indian side," Finley said, smiling softly.

"Yes, I am. I guess it seems strange to you."

"No." Finley shook her head. "At Harvard they actually had classes on alternative medicines and holistic therapies. It's very interesting; I've just never had the time to really look into it."

Kai nodded. "Well, I use it a lot in my training, making rubs for people for aches and pains and that kind of thing… and also to help them with issues like digestion or kidney troubles like mine."

"And this oil absorbs through the skin," Finley clarified.

"Right. It's not that junk oil you can buy anywhere—this stuff is very specifically grown and harvested for holistic uses. It's designed to even be ingested."

"Really?"

Kai nodded. "Yep."

"And that book is…" Finley said, looking at the spiral-bound book in Kai's hands.

"Is a kind of guide to what oils can be used for what issues."

Finley nodded, looking at Kai, her eyes softening. "And you're using it to make me feel better. Wait, where did you get this?"

"Well, the book was in my car, but the rest I picked up down at that market."

"You bought all those oils?" Finley asked, having seen the small satchel Kai was keeping them in—it looked significant.

"I have a much bigger one at home," Kai said, grinning.

Finley shook her head. "I'm going to make you go broke."

"Oh, I doubt that."

"I don't—you're forever spending money on me," Finley said, looking abashed.

"Stop it," Kai said softly. "I'm taking care of my girl, and that's worth every penny I have."

Finley pressed her lips together, warmed by Kai's words and too tired to continue to try and argue with her. She lay quietly in the tub for a while. At one point she opened her eyes. Kai's head was bent as she studied the book. A few strands of her long black hair had escaped the ponytail and hung loosely around her face.

"You are so gorgeous," Finley said softly.

Kai looked up at her, smiling. "Thanks. You're pretty hot yourself."

"Oh yeah, I'm sure I am right now. My nose has got to be completely red…"

"Just a little, and it's cute," Kai said, winking.

"You need so much help…" Finley said, shaking her head.

Kai just grinned engagingly.

They spent the next two days much the same way. On the second day, Riley showed up at the apartment to check on her daughter. She was shocked when Kai answered the door.

"Kai," Riley said, staring up at the other woman. "What are you doing here?"

"Finley's sick," Kai said matter-of-factly.

"And you're taking care of her?" Riley asked, as if she couldn't believe it.

"Of course."

Riley walked through the condo and could smell varied scents. When she went into her daughter's room she saw a diffuser running next to the bed. Finley was sitting up in her bathrobe, with a cup in her hands. She didn't look up when her mother came in, assuming it was Kai.

"I'm drinking, I promise," Finley said, grinning as she glanced up. "Oh, Mom, hi."

"I called the hospital to talk to you and Jacks said you were sick," Riley said, sitting on the bed.

"And you ran right over here to check on me?" Finley asked wryly, even as she saw Kai shake her head behind Riley.

"Don't be like that, Finley, it's not becoming," Riley said, reaching up to brush a curl off her daughter's cheek.

Finley caught Kai's look and blew her breath out slowly, refusing to rise to her mother's bait.

"So Kai's taking care of you?" Riley said after a few long moments of silence.

"Yep," Finley said, smiling at Kai. "Best bedside manner I've ever seen," she added with a wink at her.

"Is she being a good patient?" Riley asked over her shoulder.

"She's being a great patient, dutifully drinking whatever I give her."

"And she's running baths for me, and making me chicken soup from scratch…"

"Wow," Riley said, glancing back at Kai. "I'm thinking I need to change teams for sure now…"

"Well, too bad—Kai's mine," Finley said with a grin.

Kai smiled at Finley, happy to see she wasn't getting mad at her mother.

"I could thumb-wrestle you for her," Riley said.

"Nope!" Finley said. "She's mine, I'm keeping her, and besides, you cheat at thumb-wrestling."

"I do not!" Riley said, sounding aghast as she chuckled. "Okay, maybe a little." She winked at Kai. "Strong thumbs," she said, like it was the sexiest thing on the Earth.

Kai grinned. "I'll keep that in mind."

Riley left a little while later, telling Kai to keep up the good work to get "our girl" better. Kai said she'd do her damndest.

"I do believe you will," Riley said, running her finger over Kai's jaw with a smile. "I think you are the best thing my daughter has ever been lucky enough to find. I hope she holds on to you."

"Oh, she's got me pretty good," Kai said, smiling.

Riley nodded. "Good."

As Kai had promised, she took care of Finley. She was there constantly to feed her, make her tea, run her baths, and hold her when she slept or was cold. On the third day, Finley woke feeling better. Kai was asleep, so she was able to stare up at her unobserved. Finley found that she loved looking at Kai while she slept, the way her long black lashes lay against her cheeks, her lips slightly parted…

When Kai stirred and opened her eyes, she could see right away that Finley was feeling better.

"Hi," Finley said, her eyes sparkling.

"Hi," Kai replied, leaning down to kiss her softly. "How are you feeling?"

Finley smiled. "Better, thanks to you."

"Better is the important part," Kai said, grinning.

Finley reached out, touching Kai's cheek. "Thank you for this, for taking care of me," she said softly.

"It's been my pleasure. Thank you for letting me take care of you—like you did for me when I was sick."

"It's not a contest, you know," Finley said, smiling.

"No, but it is a relationship. And you do that for each other in a relationship."

Finley looked back at Kai and thought she couldn't believe how lucky she'd gotten in finding her. The woman was amazing.

Their lives got back to somewhat normal shortly after that. Kai even went with Finley to Natalia's class, since she needed to talk to Dakota and see the progress on the gym space. When the two of them walked into the studio together, there were a lot of smiles and nods. Of course, everyone had long since heard about them being a couple, but it was the first time they'd arrived somewhere together. Natalia quickly called the class to order and beckoned Finley out onto the floor. Meanwhile the bois all grinned and nodded to Kai, who shook her head, suddenly realizing what it was like to be part of the group for real. She'd known that Remi, Wynter, Quinn, Xandy, Memphis, and Kieran had been rooting for her to get together with Finley, but she hadn't realized how pleased everyone else was.

As the class started, Kai found her attention drawn to Finley. Within minutes Kai was fascinated, watching her move.

"How the hell did I ever miss her?" she asked Remington.

"Too busy to pay close attention?" Remington suggested.

Kai shook her head. "Now I know why you all love Natalia so much," she said, grinning as she caught Finley's eye.

"She does make our girls look damned good," Quinn put in.

"I'm thinking I need to send Natalia flowers," Kai said.

"Trust me, we've all thought that a few times," Jericho said from behind them.

Kai chuckled.

Later, on the way home, Kai looked over at Finley. She grinned. "You looked… um… damned good out there…"

"Did I?"

"Uh-huh," Kai said, her look pointed.

"I noticed you only got part of your workout in."

"Well, I was a bit distracted…"

"So maybe we need to make sure you work out some more…" Finley said, letting her voice trail off seductively.

"Sounds like a good idea."

"Is Cass spending the night over at Quinn and Xandy's?"

"I believe she is."

"Nice… that means we can be as noisy we want."

"Yes, it does…"

Back at Kai's house, Kai made dinner while Finley showered. After they ate, Kai took her turn. While Kai was in the bathroom, Finley lit candles in the bedroom. When Kai got out of the shower, she could smell the scent. She hadn't washed her hair, because she hadn't sweated enough to worry about it. After she dried off, she walked out to the bedroom and was pleasantly surprised to find Finley waiting for her on the bed, completely naked.

"Well," Kai said, smiling. "Is it my birthday and I forgot?" she asked, her dark eyes sparkling.

"No, I just want you and don't want to waste time with clothes…"

Kai climbed onto the bed, leaning down to claim Finley's lips with hers. She spent what seemed like hours kissing Finley, slowly and deliberately. Finley's hands slid over Kai's skin, pulling at her to bring her down to her body, but Kai didn't move. She was taking her time, and Finley was beside herself with desire.

Finally Kai lay down behind Finley, who was on her side. Finley started to turn over to face her, but Kai stopped her.

"Stay right there," Kai said against her ear.

"What—" Finley began, but then Kai's hands slid around her, touching both Finley's nipples at the same time. She gasped.

Kai began kissing Finley's neck, her fingers fondling and exciting Finley more and more. She nipped at Finley's skin, making her jump as anticipation shot through her.

"Kai, please…"

Kai slid her hand down to Finley's waist, holding her close as she rolled onto her back so Finley lay on top of her, her back to Kai's chest.

"What are you—" Finley started, but Kai's hands on her nipples again stayed her questions.

She was further shocked when one of Kai's hands moved down, hovering just above her pubic hair, and Finley was sure she was going to explode with the desire to have Kai touch her. She squirmed against Kai, pressing her body closer.

Kai continued to suck and bite at Finley's neck, while her hands continued their ministrations, never actually touching Finley where she really wanted it most.

"Kai, please… please… I want you so much… please…"

She was surprised but completely turned on when she felt Kai move her legs to hook her knees, spreading her legs with her own. Finley was sure she was going to explode—she was vibrating with desire. When Kai finally slid her fingers into her warm, moist heat, Finley began coming immediately.

"Fuck me, Kai, please fuck me…" she groaned.

Kai's long fingers sliding inside her made her come again, screaming and rubbing herself against Kai so hard Kai came as well. Even after the first couple of times, Kai continued to touch Finley, making her come again and again. When Finley was exhausted, Kai rolled them both to their sides, snuggling against Finley's back.

"That's how I wanted to top you," Kai whispered against Finley's neck.

Finley sighed softly. "You can top me like that any time you want."

Kai grinned against Finley's skin. "I love you," she said, her voice almost a sigh.

Finley turned over, looking up at her. "You do?" she asked, her tone wondrous.

"I think I have since the hospital. I just didn't say it because I thought it would freak you out."

Finley nodded. "It probably would have."

Kai nodded, leaning in to kiss Finley's lips again, noting that Finley hadn't returned the declaration and doing her best not to be hurt by that. She knew it was still early in their relationship and that Finley didn't share her philosophy of everything happening for a reason.

Kai honestly felt that Finley had been put into her life for a reason, and that they'd been meant for each other. She knew it was crazy, but she knew how she felt, and she was ready to settle into a life with Finley. There was always that stigma with lesbians that they moved quickly; the fact was, Kai hadn't ever moved so quickly in her life, which was what made her feel that things were right with Finley.

They kissed for a while and ended up falling asleep facing each other.

The next morning Finley woke to find that Kai was already up. She glanced at the clock on the nightstand. It was only five in the morning—the sun wasn't even up yet. Knowing Kai was an early riser, Finley didn't think much of it. She settled back into sleep for another hour. Waking up again, she pulled on a pair of sweats, a T-shirt, and one of Kai's fleece jackets, and walked through the house looking for her. She was surprised when she spotted her sitting in the backyard, smoking. She hadn't seen Kai smoke since that first night at The Club; she'd actually forgotten about it.

Finley walked outside and slid her hands down Kai's chest from behind, leaning down to kiss her neck softly. She then sat in the chair next to Kai's, glancing over at her.

"I've only seen you smoke once," Finley said gently. She could see that Kai was tense.

Kai blew out a long stream of smoke, her eyes narrowing behind the wisps curling around her head. "I don't do it often." She knew Finley was referring to that night at The Club.

"So why are you smoking this morning?"

Kai picked up her phone, put in the code to unlock it, and handed it to Finley. "Read it," she said, her tone low.

Finley found herself looking at an email from a Terra McGinnt:

"As such that my daughter's father is unwilling to care for her, I am sending for her and would appreciate your putting her on a plane to Atatürk International Airport as soon as possible. Marou has stated he will reimburse you for the cost of the ticket. Please email me at this address to give me the information as to the date and time of her arrival."

"Who the hell is she?" Finley asked.

"Cass's mother," Kai said evenly as she took another long drag of the cigarette. "Scroll down, see where it started."

Finley scrolled down through the email chain. It had started with Marou Temple informing Terra McGinnt that Cassiana's sister had requested to take over custody of Cassiana and that she should be aware that Kai was highly unsuitable as a parental figure as she led an alternative lifestyle that was in direct opposition to his personal beliefs. He'd gone on to offer to pay child support to Terra if she took over the care of their daughter.

"That son of a bitch…" Finley muttered. "And of course she went for it, right? Because that's what it's about for her."

Kai nodded, her teeth clenched. "Like she's a fucking piece of meat to be bargained over."

"Oh, Kai… I'm so sorry," Finley said, setting the phone down and looking over at her.

She couldn't even fathom what was going through Kai's head at that point. For her father to betray her that way and refer to her as "unsuitable" had to hurt deeply. On top of that, for her father and Cassiana's mother to completely disregard Cassiana's needs or desires in the matter was reprehensible at best.

"What are you going to do?" Finley asked softly.

Kai narrowed her eyes. "What can I do? I can't let Cass down— I have to fight them."

Finley nodded, reaching out to touch Kai's arm. "Are you okay?"

Kai stared straight ahead, looking somewhat dazed. "I guess a lousy mother is better than a gay sister in Marou's book," she said, her tone barely belying the hurt she felt. "I'll never be good enough for him," she added, her expression pained. "I guess part of me always knew that—it's just hard having it proven."

Finley was at a loss as to what to say. She knew there wasn't much she could do.

Later that morning, when Cassiana came back from Quinn and Xandy's, Kai suggested they take the dogs to the beach. Cassiana could tell there was something wrong. Kai had the stereo on loud and turned up the song; it was "Good Enough," with Jussie Smollett singing about trying to please a father who would never accept him because he was gay.

The line "I try to show you that I'm strong, why do I even bother? 'Cause it's the same old damn song, and you call yourself a father" resonated deeply with both women.

At the beach, Kai let the boys run, throwing them balls and letting them wear themselves out. After a while, she leaned against the grill of the Navigator and lit a cigarette. Cassiana knew for sure then that there was a problem.

"What is it, KaiMarou?" she asked, feeling stressed.

Kai looked over at her, thinking how completely unfair life was sometimes. She blew her breath out, knowing she needed to tell Cassiana what was happening.

"Our father saw fit to contact your mother to let her know about my asking for custody of you," she began, and Cassiana knew instantly that this was going to be very bad.

"Why?"

Kai gave a short, humorless laugh. "Because I'm 'unsuitable as a parental figure,'" she said, using air quotes.

"Has he looked in a mirror lately?" Cassiana asked snidely.

"Well, he's not gay, so… Apparently that automatically makes someone more suitable than me," Kai said, her tone almost a growl.

Cassiana shook her head. "My mom doesn't want me—it's not

going to matter."

"Oh, it matters," Kai said bleakly. "Because Marou also offered to continue to pay her child support in the amount of two thousand dollars a month if she'll take you back."

"What!" Cassiana exclaimed, paling significantly. "He can't do that!"

Kai's lips curled in a derisive smile. "Sadly, yes, he can."

Cassiana looked back at Kai, her mouth hanging open, her eyes filling with tears.

"I don't want to live with her, Kai," she said tearfully. "I want to live with you. Why don't they care about that?"

Kai grimaced. The fact was that neither of Cassiana's parents cared what she wanted or what was best for her. Cassiana threw her arms around Kai, crying almost hysterically for a few minutes. Kai held her little sister, feeling like crap and wishing things were different.

"I won't go," Cassiana said, shaking her head. "I'll run away before I'll go to her, Kai."

"You're not running away," Kai said, shaking her head. "I'm going to fight this."

"How?"

"I've already called my lawyers and they're going to get back to me with my options. I'm not giving you up without a fight, Cass, okay? As long as you still want to live with me…"

"I do! You're the only one that's ever cared about me, Kai. My life is so much better here with you. I can't live with her, or him… I can't…"

Kai nodded. "Okay, well, first I have to answer your mother. She wants me to put you on a plane like now."

Cassiana bit her lip, her eyes wide, then started to grin. "You know, I don't know what I did with my passport. I think I lost it…"

Kai started to grin. "Really? Well, damn. We're going to have to apply for a replacement before I can send you to Turkey."

"Rats," Cassiana said, grinning too.

Kai pulled Cassiana into her arms, hugging her close and kissing the top of her head. "I love you, and I'm not letting you go so easy. They're going to have to get a court order to force me."

Cassiana hugged Kai hard, so glad she'd found her sister and that she'd turned out to be such an awesome person.

Later that day Kai's lawyers came back with news that wasn't so great. In essence Kai had no real claim to Cassiana for custody. They said that Kai could try to make a case for emotional abuse on the part of Cassiana's mother, and also emotional abandonment from their father, but it wasn't a sure thing. And it wouldn't stop Terra McGinnt from insisting that Kai send Cassiana to her immediately. They also told her that if a lengthy custody battle ensued, Kai's life would be examined closely for stability in Cassiana's home life. The lawyer asked her if she was seeing someone. Kai said she was and that the woman was a doctor.

"That would be perfect. Is she living with you?" the lawyer asked.

"Uh, no. We've only been together about three months."

"Hmm… living with you would be better—then we can say that

Cassiana has a stable home environment with two parental figures."

Kai told Finley this later that night when Finley got off work. Kai picked her up at the hospital, which had become habit whenever Finley was going to stay at the house versus her condo, which was almost every night. Kai didn't want her wasting money on Uber; Finley found it endearing.

"So they just want me to move in to make things look good?" Finley asked, thinking lawyers never bothered with the feelings involved, just making it look good.

Kai grinned. "Well, yeah, that's basically what they said... but..."

"But what?"

"Well, the fact is you're here most nights now anyway..."

"Yeah, but that's different than moving in, Kai."

Kai gave her a look she didn't understand. "How's it different?"

"Moving in is a big step," Finley said, her tone indicating she didn't understand why Kai didn't know that.

Drawing in a slow, deep breath, Kai nodded, suddenly wanting to get out of the conversation because it was headed into dangerous territory. She reached over and turned up the stereo. Linkin Park's "Lost in the Echo" came on; the line "I can't fall back, I came too far" struck a little painfully close to home.

Kai shifted gears and flipped a U-turn in the middle of the next block. Finley knew before Kai stopped that she was taking her to her condo. She pulled up outside and sat stone-faced, waiting for Finley to get out of the car.

"Kai, can't we talk about this?" she asked, surprised by the sudden change in her.

Kai stared straight ahead. "Not much to say, is there?"

"But, Kai…"

"This is better," Kai said simply, not looking at Finley, her jaw jumping as she clenched her teeth.

Finley stared at her, suddenly feeling a knot in her stomach. She knew she was seeing a side of Kai that she'd never seen before, and she knew without a doubt that no matter what she said at that moment, nothing would change the look on Kai's face. Feeling tears stinging the backs of her eyes, Finley reached blindly for the door handle. She shut the door softly behind her, closing her eyes as she did. She knew she'd just lost Kai and instantly felt sick about it.

She heard the car pull away from the curb. Shivering, she wrapped her arms around herself as she walked into her building. She held herself together long enough to get inside the condo, but immediately went to her room and lay down on her bed, allowing herself to cry then. Her pillows still smelled like Kai, from when she'd been sick, and that made her cry harder. Her heart was breaking and she knew it.

Kai got out of her car, refusing to let herself think of Finley and what had just happened. She walked through the house, picking up her cigarettes from the box near the door, and went outside.

Cassiana found her there two hours later. It was really cold out now that winter was setting in; Kai was sleeveless and didn't seem to notice it.

"Where's Finley?" Cassiana asked cautiously.

"Her place."

"Why?" Cassiana searched Kai's face, seeing no emotion there whatsoever.

Kai shook her head.

"Did you two break up?" Cassiana asked, looking devastated by the thought.

Kai shrugged, her glance at Cassiana noncommittal. "Are you going to Quinn and Xandy's tonight?" she asked, her voice completely even.

"I can hang out here if you want me to…" Cassiana said, still looking for some kind of sign of how Kai was feeling.

Kai shook her head. "No point." She lifted another cigarette to her mouth and lit it.

Cassiana had never seen Kai like this, and had no idea what to do. She left the house a little while later, and when she got to Quinn and Xandy's, she got Remington's number from Quinn.

"What's goin' on?" Quinn asked, seeing the worried look on Cassiana's face.

"Something's wrong with Kai."

"Like what?"

"I think she and Finley broke up, but she won't tell me anything."

Quinn nodded. "Call Remi, she's probably the only one Kai'll talk to."

An hour later, Kai was still sitting in her backyard when Remington came striding around the side of the house, having vaulted the fence. Kai glanced at her, her expression reflecting only mild surprise at her appearance. Remington walked over and sat down, glancing at the ashtray on the table in front of Kai and seeing it was full of butts.

"What's goin' on?" she asked casually.

Kai gave her a measuring look. "Cass call you?"

Remington nodded. "She's worried about you."

"I'm fine."

Remington nodded again, looking unconvinced as she reached for one of Kai's cigarettes and lit it.

"That's why you're sitting out here without a jacket and looking to catch cancer?" Remington said. "What happened with Finley?"

Kai shook her head, her face completely closed off.

"Want to go to the gym and work some of this off?"

Kai looked thoughtful, then nodded and stood.

Three hours later she climbed out of Remington's GTO and staggered into her house, showered, and dropped into bed exhausted. She knew without a doubt she'd be sore as hell the next day. She woke feeling like she'd been run over by a truck, but got up, got dressed, and kept her appointments for the day. She then went back to the gym and spent another three hours abusing her body to the point of exhaustion.

Four days after the incident, Remington called Finley.

"Okay, so what happened?" Remington asked, having had no luck getting it out of Kai. She was tired of taking nasty body blows when she pushed her too hard for answers.

"What do you mean?"

"Kai's disappeared on us; a block of solid ice has replaced her. And she's beating the hell out of me every time I ask her about you."

"She told me she loved me," Finley said after a long pause.

"And you said…"

"I didn't answer her," Finley said, grimacing.

"And that's because?"

"Because, Remi, I know saying that to her is a major commitment, and I'm just not sure if I'm ready for that."

Remington winced, but nodded. "Well, you're right about the major commitment thing. You don't tell Kai you love her unless you're sure."

"I know. I know she's going to want it all if I say that, and… I just don't know… She scares the hell out of me with her intensity, Remi."

Remington was silent for a long moment. "Kai doesn't do anything halfway, Finley. You're dead on there."

"I've lost her."

Remington didn't tell her she was wrong. It broke her heart a little bit more.

One evening when Remington had finally dragged Kai out of the house and to the bar, they had the misfortune of running into Kathy. Naturally, Kathy made a beeline for Kai, having heard that Kai had been dating a doctor but that they'd broken up. She figured now was her time to strike, but this time Kai was ruthless, not willing to put up with Kathy's crap anymore. Kathy's advances fell on an utterly ice-cold Kai, and it shook her completely.

"What's wrong with you?" Kathy asked, her tone reflecting her amazement that her spell over Kai seemed to have been nullified.

Kai's lips twisted in a sarcastic grin. "I'm over you."

"You'll never be over me," Kathy snorted.

Kai looked back at her, her dark gaze unfazed. "Go away, Kathy. Go back to your wife, or to whatever fucking rock you crawled out from under. I have no use for you."

With that Kai turned to walk away. Kathy caught her arm, and Kai spun, knocking away her hand.

"You're gonna regret this," Kathy said icily. "Mark my words, I'll make you regret this."

"Go ahead and try," Kai gritted out, then turned and walked away. The fact that she was so over Kathy because of Finley rang through her head. Her heart ached at the thought as she gritted her teeth. She proceeded back over to the bar, where she drank heavily until the wee hours of the morning.

Jackie had had it with Finley's long face and refusal to talk about what had happened with Kai. It had been a week already. She called Riley, telling her about her daughter's spiraling mood. Riley swept into the ER and informed Finley that she'd be having lunch with her.

"I'm busy, Mom," Finley said, her tone completely lifeless.

"Well, Jackie's cleared your schedule. So let's go."

Finley glared at Jackie, but she simply looked back at her unwaveringly.

Riley dragged Finley to a local place where she was less likely to be recognized and had them seat them in the very back.

"Okay, you tell me now, what happened with you and Kai?" Riley asked sharply.

"It doesn't matter, Mom, it's just over," Finley said, shaking her head sadly.

"Like hell it is!" Riley exclaimed, startling the people around them. "That woman is the best damned thing that ever happened to you, and you're not giving her up without a fight."

"There was no fight—there was just… ice…"

"What happened?"

Finley looked back at her mother. "Why do you care?"

"What do you mean, why do I care?" Riley sounded shocked by the question.

"I mean, why do you care?" Finley said, suddenly finding an outlet for her anger and pain. "I mean, you've never fucking cared how I feel about anything—why do you fucking care now?"

"Where is this coming from?" Riley asked, blinking in surprise at Finley's venom.

"It's coming from the truth, Mom. Face it, you've never really given a shit about what I did as soon as I quit doing the beauty pageants, acting classes, and dance classes—when you realized I wasn't going to be your perfect little doll."

"You were a beautiful child. I wanted you to know that."

"You could have told me that. You didn't have to shove me in every director's face, every stupid pageant judge's face."

217

"Your mother is supposed to think you're beautiful—I wanted you to know that other people thought you were beautiful too. What does this have to do with Kai?"

"I never trust people," Finley said. "I never trusted you."

"Trust me to do what?" Riley asked, still reeling.

"Not to fuck things up!"

"What are you talking about?" Riley asked, aghast that Finley was being so nasty.

"Do you even remember Evan?" Finley asked, her voice softening on the man's name.

Riley looked confused. "Evan?"

Evan Keely had the kindest smile she'd ever seen, and he was smiling at her for a change, not her mother. He'd taken the time to come sit with her in her room, asking what she was reading.

"It's a medical journal," Finley said, showing him the copy of Dr. Seuss's One Fish, Two Fish, Red Fish, Blue Fish. *"I'm going to be a doctor," she informed him proudly.*

"Oh, I see," he said, smiling and nodding. "And is this your patient here?" He gestured to the stuffed bear lying on his back with a washcloth covering his lower half.

"Yes. I'm going to need to do surgery, and I need to make sure I know where to cut."

"Oh, there's going to be cutting?" he asked, looking slightly alarmed.

"Yep," Finley replied, holding up the butter knife she'd absconded

from the kitchen with when the cook wasn't looking.

"Oh, yes, I see," he said, touching the edge of the knife. "Very sharp scalpel there, Doctor."

Finley nodded, smiling up at him.

By the time Riley located Evan, he and Finley were "performing surgery" on the little bear. They both wore paper towels over their mouths like surgical masks, with shoe laces tying them to their faces.

"Evan, we're going to be late," Riley had said, tapping her expensive diamond watch.

Evan glanced down at Finley, who looked up at him expectantly. "I think we can sew him up pretty quickly, can't we, Doctor Taylor?"

"Yep!" she said, smiling broadly.

"Oh my God, I haven't thought of Evan in years," Riley said, shaking her head.

"I think about him all the time," Finley said. "I really thought he was going to last. But none of them ever did, Mom... none of them."

Riley looked back at her daughter. "Are you saying that you are mad at me because men I dated never worked out?"

"I'm saying it was a shit childhood, when I could never count on anything, not you, not them, no one—nothing."

"What happened with Kai?" Riley asked, sensing this was all somehow related.

Finley shook her head. "It doesn't matter."

Riley reached out, touching her daughter's hand. "It does matter, Finley. Your heart is broken."

Finley felt tears clog her throat as she shook her head.

"What happened?" Riley asked again.

"She told me she loved me."

"Why is that a bad thing?"

"Because I had no idea how to respond, Mom."

"The commonly accepted response is 'I love you too,' dear," Riley said drily.

"I was afraid to say that to her."

"Why?"

"Because she's so... You can't just say stuff like that to Kai—she takes it very seriously."

"What more are you looking for in a woman, Finley? Why are you letting her go?"

"Because I'm afraid I can't commit to her, Mom, like you never committed to anyone!" Finley snapped, tired of the thoughts going around and around in her head. "I need to get back to work," she said, getting up and walking blindly out of the restaurant, tears already starting in her eyes.

She made her way back to the hospital and threw herself into her work. She'd volunteered for every extra shift available. Exhaustion had already set in, but when she got a head cold she insisted on working through it, refusing to think of the time she'd been sick and Kai had taken such good care of her. Part of her knew she'd never have that again.

Meanwhile, Kai got into the routine of working and then going to the gym. She refused to stop and think of Finley and what she'd lost. Two weekends later she reported to Camp Pendleton for her monthly reserve drill weekend. There, under the guise of training plebes, she spent all of her time beating the hell out of any Marine foolhardy enough to test her.

Finley was working herself to death, so Jackie had arranged to get some time off and told Finley she wanted to do a girl's weekend with her. Finley had agreed, but only on the condition that they wouldn't talk about Kai at all. Jackie agreed begrudgingly. They drove down to San Diego and went to the beach and to some local restaurants. They had a good time, and Finley finally felt like she might be getting back to her old self.

On Sunday they drove back to Los Angeles. Jackie said she needed to go to the bathroom when they were just on the north side of Oceanside. She pulled off on the Vandegrift Boulevard exit. Finley was busy looking at some of the pictures she'd taken on her phone, so she wasn't paying attention. When Jackie pulled over into a parking lot and turned off the engine, Finley waited for her to get out to go to the bathroom. When Jackie didn't get out of the car, she looked up.

The first thing she saw was the sign for the Camp Pendleton main gate.

"Jackie…" Finley said, even as she saw soldiers walking out of the gate and coming toward the parking lot.

Finley's eyes tracked over to Jackie, and then she caught a glimpse of a car that was a very familiar shade of green.

"Jackie, what are you…" she began, and then she saw her.

Kai was wearing her Battle Dress Uniform, complete with boots and hat, her gold eagle insignia on her cap and collar, her dark hair tucked under the cap. Finley felt her insides tremble.

"Finley, you are in love with that woman," Jackie said. "And you need to go and tell her that right now."

"I can't…" Finley said, tears in her eyes as she shook her head.

"You can. And you need to, right now."

As Kai started toward her car, Finley noticed the cuts on her cheek, the bruise at her mouth. She thought about what Remington had said about Kai beating the hell out of her every time she asked Kai about her. Was she getting into fights with others now?

"She looks like she's hurting," Jackie pointed out.

Finley noticed then how stiffly Kai was moving. Concern for Kai's health and well-being kicked in, making Finley get out of the car. Kai was five feet from her. Their eyes connected instantly—it was obvious that Kai was shocked to see Finley there.

"What…" Kai began, her eyes trailing from Finley to Jackie, then back to Finley. "What are you doing here?" she asked, going to her car and opening her trunk to drop in her gear bag.

Finley walked over to Kai, looking up at her face, taking in the cuts and bruises. "What happened?"

Kai looked back at her coolly. "Training."

"Kai…" Finley began softly, even as she reached up to touch the bruise at Kai's mouth.

Kai yanked her head away, backing up against her car, a look of pain crossing her face.

"You're hurt," Finley said, reaching out to touch Kai's side.

"Don't!" Kai snapped.

Finley jumped, but touched Kai's side gently. She felt Kai jump at the contact; regardless, she carefully unbuttoned her jacket and untucked the T-shirt from the BDU pants, gathering the shirt to look at the vicious bruise on Kai's side.

"Oh my God… Kai," Finley said. "What have you done to yourself?" When she looked up, she caught the look of complete anguish in Kai's eyes.

Finley stared up at her. "Kai, I'm so sorry," she said, her voice full of the tears she was trying to hold in. "I love you. I'm so sorry—please, I love you…" She reached up to touch Kai's face, desperate to take that look out of her eyes.

Kai's lips were on hers then, and Finley felt Kai's hand on her back, her other at the back of her neck as she kissed her deeply, pouring all of the pain and sorrow of the last two weeks into it. Finley slid her arms up around Kai's neck, holding on to her desperately, afraid that letting go would mean losing her again.

In her car, Jackie smiled. "About damned time, you two," she muttered happily.

Two weeks later, Finley was living with Kai and Cassiana and her condo was up for sale. She had never been so happy in her life, and she couldn't even fathom why she had ever thought it would be different with Kai.

She stood in the kitchen early one morning as the sun was just coming up, watching through the window as Kai played with the boys, throwing them tennis balls. She could hear Kai laughing as one of the dogs did something silly. The sound warmed her heart. They'd had a long conversation about why Finley had been so slow to return Kai's admission of love, and Kai understood that it stemmed from years and years of not counting on anyone or anything. Finley understood now how much it had hurt Kai that she hadn't been able to commit to her. It had reminded Kai of Kathy and her game playing, which was why Kai had gone so cold. She'd felt played again.

Finley went outside and handed Kai a coffee, leaning up to kiss her.

"Good morning," Kai said, smiling down at her.

"Hi," Finley said, smiling back.

Kai sat on one of the chaises longues and gently pulled Finley down with her. They lay together, watching the sun rise through the canyon, Kai holding Finley against her, her lips against Finley's temple.

A few minutes after the sun rose, Kai's phone rang. She pulled it out of her pocket and looked down at the display with a grimace. It was Cassiana's mother. Finley tensed, knowing this was the call Kai had been waiting for.

Kai hit the speaker phone, wanting Finley to hear the conversation too. "Hello," she said.

"Is this Kai?" asked Terra McGinnt tentatively.

"Yes," Kai said, her tone businesslike. "Thank you for calling me back."

"When are you sending Cassiana?"

"I'm not. She's staying here with me, where she belongs."

"I don't think you fully grasp the situation here, Kai," Terra began officiously.

"Oh, I think I grasp it pretty well."

"Then you should know that I'm more than willing to involve the authorities if you—"

"How much?" Kai asked, interrupting whatever threat Terra had been about to make.

"I'm sorry?"

"I asked how much," Kai said, her tone not reflecting the disgust in her eyes.

"How much, what?"

"How much is it going to cost me to get rid of you for good?"

"I don't know what you mean," Terra said, doing her best to sound offended.

"Oh, I think you do," Kai said. "I figure my father's going to pay you two thousand a month until Cass is eighteen—that's eighteen months, so thirty-six thousand dollars. I'll give you fifty thousand if you'll sign over your parental rights to me."

There was silence on the other end of the line. Kai narrowed her eyes slightly, glancing at Finley, who was watching with concern clear on her face. They'd discussed this and Kai knew she was taking a chance approaching Terra this way; she could be charged with attempting to traffic Cassiana. Both Lyric and Cody had assured her that not too many judges would see it that way, but not before they had both offered to help Kai with however much money she needed to buy Cassiana out of Terra's clutches.

"I don't think you know how much I love my daughter," Terra said, her tone all greed now.

"Sixty," Kai said immediately.

Once again there was silence. Kai had to swallow against the bile that was rising in her throat at having to deal with this sleazy woman.

"When can you get me the money?"

"As soon as you sign the documents I'm emailing you."

"Okay. Send them."

It was as simple as that. Kai got the documents signed, and she wired a check for sixty thousand dollars. It had been a stretch, since much of her money was tied up in investments, but it was worth every penny to get Terra out of Cassiana's life forever, and Kai had made sure the documents Terra signed ensured that. She was never to contact Kai, Cassiana, Marou, or any member of the Temple family again. If Cassiana decided later that she wanted contact with her mother, she had that option.

Three nights later, Kai escorted Finley to her mother's fundraiser, wearing a very well-tailored tuxedo with a burgundy tie that matched Finley's dress. Kai's appearance left Finley absolutely verklempt and speechless.

"Oh my God," Finley said, reaching up to put her hands on Kai's shoulders. "You look so handsome."

"No, you need to just stand there and let me look at you," Kai said, stepping back from Finley, her dark eyes sparkling. "Fin... God, you are so beautiful." She touched Finley's cheek. "You are literally the most beautiful woman I have ever seen... and I love you."

"Thank you. I love you," she said, smiling brightly up at Kai.

They made quite a stir at the fundraiser, an extremely beautiful couple with Kai's dark looks and Finley the classic California blonde in her incredible dress.

At one point they slow-danced to Adele's "Lovesong." Finley sang the words to the first verse to Kai.

Kai leaned down, kissing Finley's lips, and proceeded to sing the chorus to her.

"I will always love you," Kai said, mimicking the chorus.

Finley hugged Kai close, not sure how she'd gotten so lucky to have found her, lost her, and gotten her back—but she knew she would hold on to this woman forever, come what may.

Epilogue

Kai and Finley were asleep when Cassiana knocked on their door.

Kai groaned, glancing at the clock on the nightstand. It was 6 a.m.; normally she'd be awake, but they'd gone out the night before, staying out late.

"Yeah?" Kai called, after checking to make sure she and Finley were covered.

Cassiana stuck her head in the door. "I'm sorry to wake you, but Fin's mom's here…"

"What?" Finley said, having heard. "Why is my mom here?" she queried to no one in particular.

"She said she needs to talk to Kai," Cassiana said.

Kai and Finley looked at each other. "Okay, Cass, I'll be out in a minute," Kai said.

Cassiana nodded, closing the door. She walked back down the hall, doing her best not to be completely dazzled by the Academy Award–winning actress standing in the foyer, but it was really hard. Even without makeup and in jeans and a sweater, Riley Taylor was amazingly beautiful.

"Kai'll be out in a minute," Cassie said, staring at the actress.

"Great, thank you," Riley said, smiling her dazzling movie star smile.

"Um, did you want some coffee or something?"

Riley nodded. "Sure."

"Okay," Cassiana said, and led the way to the kitchen.

She carefully poured for Riley, handing her the coffee without spilling any, even though her hands were shaking. She'd never met a movie star before. Sure, she'd met Xandy Blue and Wynter, but she knew them now, and they weren't as famous as Riley Taylor. Riley Taylor had been in movies forever! Cassiana had grown up watching her movies and loving her to death. She was still so beautiful it was crazy.

Riley looked at Cassiana, seeing the way the girl was staring at her. She was used to it; people stared at her all the time.

"So you're Kai's baby sister, right?" she asked.

Cassiana nodded. "Only sister."

"But she's your guardian?"

"Right. 'Cause my parents suck. Oh!" She grimaced. "I'm sorry."

Riley laughed. "It's okay, lots of parents suck. I think my daughter probably says I suck all the time."

"I do not," Finley said, walking into the kitchen. "Okay, I have a couple of times, but you're starting to grow on me," she added with a wink.

Kai walked in behind Finley, reaching over to hug Riley.

"Good morning," Kai said, looking for coffee mugs for her and Finley and pouring for them both.

"Hi, sorry to get you out of bed," Riley said, grimacing. "I thought you always got up early—at least, that's what Finley told me."

"I usually do. We stayed out late last night," Kai said, winking at Finley.

Riley smiled. "Oh, I see…"

"Let's sit," Kai said, gesturing to the kitchen table. The three of them sat down, Cassiana hovering near the kitchen counter.

"So what's up?" Finley asked her mother. "Why'd you want to see Kai?"

"I need her help," Riley said, looking from Finley to Kai. "And I'm begging here, and I'll pay you anything you want."

Kai grinned. "Tell me what we're talking about first."

"I need you to train me," Riley said, holding up her hand as Finley started to shake her head.

"Mom, Kai's got a waiting list a mile long," Finley said, "and it's only getting longer every time someone sees BJ Sparks on stage and hears that she trained him for this tour."

Riley nodded. "I know, I know. But this is really important to me—it's not just vanity now."

"Tell me what's up," Kai said, putting her hand on Finley's to silence her defense.

"There's a part that I want more than any part I've wanted in more years than I can even count at this point, but I need to be in top shape to even try for it."

"What's the part?" Finley asked, not having heard her mother this excited about a role in a while now.

"It's a part in the first movie that Legend Azaria has written and is now directing."

"Legend Azaria?" Finley asked, having heard the name a few times over the years.

"Yes." Riley nodded excitedly. "She's the hottest director in Hollywood right now, and everyone is dying to get into this movie. I need this part!"

Kai looked between the two women. "Who's Legend Azaria?" she asked. "Apart from being 'the hottest director,' blah, blah, blah," she said, rolling her eyes. She was never impressed with Hollywood all that much.

"You'd like her, babe," Finley said, grinning. "She was a Marine."

"I don't automatically like someone because they were a Marine," Kai said, giving Finley a narrowed look.

Finley pressed her lips together, grinning. "She's gay too. And very, very butch."

Kai gave Finley a deadpan look. "Really?" she said, her tone indicating that Finley was being far too general.

"Look, that's what the movie is about," Riley said. "It's kind of autobiographical, and that's why it's literally the hottest property in town right now. I have got to get on this film! But she's never even going to look at me if I don't have something to offer. So…"

"So you want me to train you," Kai said.

Riley suddenly looked hesitant. "Not just train me…"

"Then what?" Kai asked, perplexed.

"I need you to teach me to be a Marine."

Kai laughed loudly, shaking her head. Riley Taylor was the quintessential movie star, with her long, painted nails, makeup, long hair curled just so, perfect tan—she wasn't even the beginning of a Marine. Suddenly she realized that both Riley and Finley were looking at her very seriously.

"You're kidding me, right?" Kai said, holding up her hands.

"No," Riley said, shaking her head. "I'm as serious as a heart attack right now."

"And a heart attack is likely what you'll have if I train you."

Riley reached out, taking Kai's hands, feeling the strength in them just from her grip. "Kai, please. You're the only one that can get me ready for this. Please!"

Kai shook her head, her expression indicating that she thought Riley was crazy. "I can't train you to be a Marine, Riley. It's not something that happens overnight."

"I have six weeks," Riley said.

Kai laughed again, shaking her head. "Impossible."

"I don't know..." Finley said, giving Kai a pointed look. "I've seen my mom throw herself into a part before, and it's pretty amazing. She might be able to do it."

Kai looked cynically from Finley to Riley, then started to shake her head again.

"I'll pay you whatever you ask," Riley said.

"Riley, it's not about the money. No offense, but you're fifty years old, and far from in the shape you'd need to be for a Marine."

"She doesn't have to be a Marine, babe—she just has to play one on screen," Finley said, grinning.

Kai pursed her lips, her gaze surveying Riley's body.

"You could do it, Kai," Finley said, catching her mother's excitement now. "And just think, if you trained her for this part... It's a Legend Azaria film—it's likely to win multiple Academy Awards, and everything that woman touches turns to gold. You'd be responsible for training the woman that won an Academy Award."

Kai narrowed her eyes at Finley. "You aren't helping..."

"Kai, I will do whatever you say," Riley pleaded. "I will work my ass off, I promise you that. I can do this, I know I can!"

"Six weeks," Kai said.

"Yeah," Riley said. "That's when she's going to start casting, and I have to be ready to show her what I can do."

"You'd have to commit at least four hours a day. And you'd have to eat completely clean, no garbage, no alcohol, no smoking..."

Riley nodded excitedly. "Anything you say. Anything."

Kai's expression was deadly serious. "Just remember you said that."

Follow the author and find out more about her series here:

Website: www.sherrylhancock.com

Facebook: @SherrylDHancock

Twitter: @Sherryl_Hancock

Also by Sherryl D. Hancock:

The *MidKnight Blue* series. Dive into the world of Midnight Chevalier and as we follow her transformation from gang leader to cop from the very beginning.

www.vulpine-press.com/midknight-blue-series

The *Wild Irish Silence* series. Escape into the world of BJ Sparks and discover how he went from the small-town boy to the world-famous rock star.

www.vulpine-press.com/wild-irish-silence-series

CPSIA information can be obtained
at www.ICGtesting.com
Printed in the USA
BVHW032359121118
532989BV00003B/15/P